PRAISE FOR STEPHANIE HAN

Stephanie Han is a gifted storyteller who channels the voices of those living on the margins, between cultures, and across borders with rare understanding and skill...The vulnerabilities, flaws, neuroses, desperation, and madness of human beings left to fend for themselves on bitter and foreign soil are laid bare with quiet, charged precision. I am full of admiration for this writer and her impressive gifts.

— Gail Vida Hamburg, *The Edge of the World*

Compelling, moving and keenly observed, *Swimming in Hong Kong* is the work of a brilliant writer with a sharp eye for uncomfortable truths.

— Julie Koh, author of *Portable Curiosities* and editor of
BooksActually's Gold Standard

Stephanie Han shows us the world, especially the world of sex and romance, through the eyes of mostly women of Korean descent but of various ages and backgrounds. Sometimes savvy, and sometimes so vulnerable and naive that we cringe for them, these are characters readers will find themselves rooting for.

— Elaine H. Kim, Professor of Asian American and Asian Diaspora Studies,
UC Berkeley

In this poignant, bitter-sweet, sometimes playful, collection, *Swimming in Hong Kong*, the characters are in search of home, identity, love, respect... Their interactions and intermingling are often full of confusion and misunderstanding as they deal with issues of history, culture, religion, family, displacement, identity. The reader is enlightened as the characters try to cope with complex issues in their lives. The settings are full of striking details. The tone and voice, are varied and engaging.

— Nahid Rachlin, Judge of the 2015 AWP Grace Paley Prize for Short Fiction

At the crossroads of culture, at the intersection of being an insider and an outsider in both the US and Asia, the stories in Stephanie Han's *Swimming in Hong Kong* shimmer with a mordant wit, a sly humor, and an oblique sadness... At once novel and familiar, political and personal, these stories resonate with the kind of questions and truths that anyone who has ever felt out of his or her element will immediately understand.

— Vanina Marsot, author of *Foreign Tongue* and *The Circassian Woman*

Stephanie Han's *Swimming in Hong Kong* captures the struggle of living between cultures and between identities. Like the people in W.G. Sebald's books, Stephanie's characters live in exile and don't quite know what to do with themselves. Filled with humor and heartbreak, these stories always feel true and smart.

— Jason Brooks Brown, author of *Driving the Heart and Other Stories*,
and *Why the Devil Chose New England for His Work*

SWIMMING IN HONG KONG

SWIMMING IN HONG KONG
Stories by **Stephanie Han**

WILLOW SPRINGS BOOKS

ACKNOWLEDGEMENTS

I would like to thank my parents, Tai-June and Marie Ann Yoo, for their love and faith, and the extended Han and Yoo families for their aloha and han.

My sojourn to Seoul, Korea was filled with the laughter and insight of Andreas Bruech, Hyun Sook Leem, Jolena James-Szanton, and Cecilia Yoo.

Writers that matter: Vanina Marsot—for determined grace, Jane Chi Hyun Park—for expatriate perspectives, and Renee Simms—for words and edits.

The following provided financial assistance: PEN-West Emerging Voices, San Francisco State University Graduate Equity Fellowship, University of Arizona Asian American Faculty, Staff, and Alumni Association, and VONA.

I am so very grateful to Christopher Howell, Willow Springs Books and Eastern Washington University for publishing this book, and to Lauren Hohle for her work during the publication process.

Finally, my greatest thanks to Keohi Ki-Chan Aldred-Yoo and to Stephen John Charles Aldred: Here's to the journey we have taken together, and to the one that continues to unfold.

Stories in this collection have been previously published in the following journals:

Feminist Studies Journal: "The Body Politic, 1982"

Kyoto Journal: "Invisible" and "The Ki Difference"

The Louisville Review: "Canyon"

New Asian Short Stories: "My Friend Faith, 1977"

Nimrod International Journal of Prose and Poetry, Katherine Anne Porter Prize for Fiction: "Languages"

Santa Fe Writer's Project and *The South China Morning Post* Short Fiction Prize Winner: "Rebound"

Women's Studies Quarterly and *Cheers to Muses: Contemporary Works by Asian American Women*: "The Ladies of Sheung Wan"

Queen of Statue Square: Hong Kong Short Fiction Anthology: "Swimming in Hong Kong"

FIRST EDITION
Cover Art: Fan Yang-Tsung, *Swimming Pool Series - Tiny Pool,* 80 x 60 cm, Acrylic on canvas, 2015.
Author Photo: Kalei Simms
Cover Design: Clarinda Simpson
Interior Design: Lauren Hohle
LIBRARY OF CONGRESS CATALOGING-IN-PUBLICATION
Names: Han, Stephanie, author.
Title: Swimming in Hong Kong/written by Stephanie Han
Description: First edition. | Spokane, WA : Willow Springs Books, [2016]Indentifiers: LCCN 2016952473 | ISBN 9780983231769 (softcover : acid-free paper)

for Mom and Dad
and Stephen

TABLE OF CONTENTS

INVISIBLE

This is how to become invisible in Hong Kong. Ideally you should look Han Chinese, which is to have fair skin with dark hair and flat high cheekbones. You should be attractive, but not so much that you gain attention in any unusual way, but attractive enough to pass the scrutiny of the doorman of the club that you and your tall, light, green-eyed husband have belonged to for the past three months. You should be able to smile and flash your membership card and pull open the brass handles of the door without being stopped.

You are not a *gweilo*, a foreign devil, or a ghost person, a term of insult, but a foreigner of another kind. Your complexion is not olive, a sign to the doorman that you could be Filipina, which in most places in this city guarantees a disparaging glance, harsh words from the locals, and a lascivious glance if you are younger, by Western men who are twice your age or at least twice your body weight. You aren't Han Chinese; you are Korean.

You are seen as belonging to the local Chinese if your husband is absent and you are silent, and to the expatriates only if you are on his arm—your husband called either more or less of a man because he is with you.

This establishment is in the grand tradition of colonial clubs, yet with modern considerations. It's open to locals of a certain privilege and distinction who circulate in the company of foreigners, locals who move seamlessly from one society to the next, occupy important posts, possess substantial holdings, educate their children in the West, and who, along with their former colonial overlords, now agree with everything Beijing has to say; before everyone agreed with everything London had to say, as to agree is to be rich, which is to be glorious. It is a marvelous circle, the elite of one nation admiring and mimicking the elite of another, the mutual goal of keeping the underlings out, whatever their pigmentation, cementing the tacit bond of wealth.

You speak far less Cantonese than your British spouse, who has lived here before and rattles away words and phrases with relative ease. Your vocabulary is limited to pleasantries, basic greetings and taxicab language, and the phrase *Ngo hai han gwok yan*—I'm Korean, a sentence that has more than once smoothed your path. You have been mistaken for Japanese, and the older local generation, like people everywhere in the world, blame the sins of the past on those of the present and have greeted you with a suspicious glance. What did your relatives do to my relatives?

After going to the gym downstairs, you sit alone at the bar and order a beer. It's the beginning of a long weekend. You wait for your husband to get off of his late-night shift. You both work as journalists, neither of you with much relish or interest. In the end, it is a tree pulped for paper information that spins the cycle of money. He works for a financial mag, you for a society rag, documenting respectively the deals the husbands make that afford the jewels their wives wear. Like many other expatriates in Hong Kong, you are here to save money, to escape the West, and will eventually leave. There is little in your apartment. A single burner. A shelf of books. A holiday photo. Your clothes fit into one suitcase. You are surrounded by second-hand furniture and in the center of your home is what you have deemed the hemisphere's ugliest leather sofa, trimmed in brass and a color that is not quite beige and not quite caramel, a color that alludes to a shade of human flesh stuffed and sculpted into a form more appropriate for a Las Vegas brothel's reception area.

You call Hong Kong home when you return from holiday, but you think of the U.S. as your country, though you often wonder why, since after four generations, people there still tell you to go back to where you came from, or think it's a compliment to say that you're as good as an American, as good as a white person. Your husband calls it home because home is where he lives at the moment, and he was glad to leave the U.S., for why should he live in an expanding empire having loathed and fled a dying one? Hong Kong holds your curiosity insomuch as it was where you had met five years before and it was a place of the unexpected. The unusual. You cannot speak the language, so are cut off from the locals. You haven't had much social success with other expatriates, though this is the fault of your own actions. This is a city of bankers. Many of them bore you. And you, not being particularly interested in money, bore them. Hong Kong is a stopover. You have thoughts of other countries and don't wish to return to the U.S., not yet. You want to escape from the smog for a few days or maybe years, but have no other specific destination in mind. Like any city once you have adjusted to its rhythms and smells and beats, Hong Kong has become monotonous.

You were glad to come back to Asia. Sink into a crowd. Get lost. You are not a rugged individual. You like the anonymity. Together with your husband in the U.S. you were thought of as too yellow, too white, too privileged, too educated, too foreign, too poor, too rich, too loud, too quiet, too American, too Asian, too European. You and your husband occupy that space in between. You have what the far left and the far right seem to uncannily agree is undesirable and problematic: a mixed marriage.

You feel the room's cigarette smoke coat your skin, and sip on your beer. You look at the photographs on the wall of old Hong Kong and ponder the past year and what it has brought. Money in the bank. A dull job. A few published stories. Your marriage has weathered the move well. Between the two of you, over the past five years, you have inhabited four apartments in three cities and have moved countries twice. You know that you and the man you have married will be doing this the rest of your lives. This moving from country to country is what you share with others here. In this way, if in no other, you are a typical Hong Kong expat. You would like to find a country to belong to. A continent. You think of small tropical islands and crowded cities. You hope to find The Place to Live but have started to believe that it doesn't exist.

People are drinking. The bar is busy. Everyone is talking but on one side of you the barstool is empty, and on the other, a very tall man is arguing with his neighbor. Across the room you see an English friend of your husband's, an acquaintance to you. You have met him three times before in the U.S., once with his wife with whom your husband does not get along. You found this man pleasant, but not particularly interesting. The couple did not come to your wedding, though they were invited. He plays soccer, or rather football, with your husband and occasionally they share a beer afterwards. Once long ago, they were better friends, but they are older and their friendship is based on a past familiarity as opposed to a current compatibility.

You have seen this fellow several times since arriving. Once at a large group dinner days after your plane first landed in Hong Kong, once for a champagne brunch at a fancy hotel, and once at an early morning football game where you watched your silver-haired husband, in his late thirties, who still has the physique and the anger of a man years younger, run across the field in intense pursuit of a ball.

If you were with your husband, this man across the bar would fast approach with a greeting. But tonight you are alone, and as you have experienced at various times around the city, your English husband's presence or absence determines your status. You are elevated or lowered depending on the circumstance. You are seen or you simply disappear.

You stand up and venture a friendly wave at the man and he looks right at you, straight in the eye, but doesn't respond. He didn't see you. Or did he? You wave again, more urgently. Why, you don't know. You feel foolish and wonder if anyone else saw you wave. You slink to the back of the bar, hop up on a stool and let your right foot, with the big blister on your toe, slide out of your worn leather flat.

You smile at a few faces in the crowd—no one speaks to you but the bartenders who take your order and remember your face from prior visits. They are Chinese. The bar is crowded with Westerners. You count: four Chinese men in suits and silk ties at a corner table drinking—they smile when you walk past to go to the restroom; one Filipina woman with square shoulders at the bar with a red-haired Western man; one bearded Eurasian with naturally wavy hair and skinny limbs—you have seen him all over Central at various spots from the hours of 6:00 p.m. to 4:00 a.m. but have never met and hope you never will; a pair of older Chinese women lost in a cloud of cigarette smoke. There are Asians sitting at the table, and you are trying to decide if you should move to that area. You decide to stay for lack of incentive to move, other than to be less conspicuous, which you have felt in Hong Kong, as there are times when you have found yourself the only Asian in a room of expatriates, a situation you understand, yet find peculiar in Asia. You think you shouldn't have come alone. You have long since passed the days when you sidled up to a bar on your own and enjoyed casual drunken conversation. You are here because you want a drink after a day spent analyzing the latest designer handbags. You remember your editor's squeals of delight over the newest Gucci wallet.

—Yes, the red one is very nice, you said looking at the letter 'G' scattered all over the fabric.

You wondered how many people have the letter 'G' in their name—Geraldine, Gwyneth, Gigi, Gabby. Garrett, Guo, Gilpin, Gillotte. You cannot think of too many names with the letter 'G' and ponder why individuals buy wallets with initials that aren't their own. You think about the letter 'X' and its appeal. Xylophone, x-ray, x-rated? You cannot think of any first or last names with the letter 'X'.

—It's a season must-have. Appearances are important, she said looking at your skirt.

She wants to frown but she can't because she has had Botox treatments. Her forehead never moves. For days you said things to see if you could get her forehead to move. Nothing worked, it always stayed the same. Botox is very strong.

She stared because your skirt was the wrong length. According to fashion forecasts, it will be the right length in two years. You can wait. She never says anything about the clothes you wear. Mostly because you've been buying clothes from a cardboard box at the store selling sweatshop overruns down the street from your apartment, next to the shop selling roast duck. Whatever you buy smells like roast duck and steamed rice. Nice smells, really. You wash your new clothes before you wear them to work.

—You are not the public face of the magazine, the editor once said dryly.

You didn't say anything. Her forehead didn't move.

More people have entered the bar area. Others have left. You spy the rack of periodicals by the entrance and think about reading one but know you won't do it; instead you order a second beer. The man has not approached. You think of going over and saying hello, but he is enmeshed with his friends in one of those conversations that might awkwardly stop if you did. You feel hesitant. Shy. You didn't want to sit in an empty apartment alone; you had decided it was better to be alone in a crowd. You go to the phone to call your husband. You remember how he told you with consternation that this man and his wife would be adopting a Chinese baby.

—They do not speak a word of Chinese after living here for over a dozen years. They have no Chinese friends. They say 'the Chinese this,' 'the Chinese that.' Pathetic really, your husband said with disgust.

Your husband says this is the reason their friendship has faded.

—They've been here too long. It's what happens to some English people. People live insulated lives here and become more of what they are. They're adopting a Chinese baby to save China from China. You know why? It confirms their worst feelings about China, he said.

—I'm sure that's not the only reason. It's better than the kid staying in an orphanage, you said to your husband.

—Yes.

—They won't have much of a choice with a Chinese child but to change.

—I doubt it.

You phone him during his deadline rush. You tell him you've seen this man, his friend.

—No, he has not seen me. He can't see me. I'm invisible, you say laughing and then suddenly stop.

You feel tense. You've never sat at the bar without your husband. You don't like being there alone. You notice you're now the only Asian in the club except for the waitstaff. The Asians have left. When did that happen? You think that you should have gone straight home after work.

—No, of course not. To him you're another Asian face, he says slowly. It's odd, but not really, he sighs. So who are you with?

His voice is anxious. He joined the club so you could sit in the Jacuzzi and afterwards eat a quiet meal together in a restaurant that banned cell phones from its dining room.

—No one is talking to you?

He sounds worried. He knows you don't feel relaxed in a room full of white people in Asia. You've told him you find it peculiar. Though your language, your passport, your husband, your education and everything about you says you should feel at ease in this room, you don't. You take no pleasure in Hong Kong trailblazing.

You were not an American trailblazer. You did not invent the nectarine, win an Olympic gold medal, star in a TV show, or lead Japanese American troops into battle. You hate the phrases 'overcoming odds,' 'defying stereotypes' and 'getting ahead.' You don't like the words 'assimilation', 'model minority' and 'well-adjusted.' This is why you left the U.S. You decide you should strike up a conversation, make a friend.

—It's not a big deal, I'll talk to someone.

You say this with confidence. The problem is that you don't like small talk.

—I'll talk to someone, you say again.

Your husband does not believe you.

—I have sixty stories in front of me. I can't be there now.

He sounds upset. You realize you shouldn't have called him.

—I know, it's not a big deal, really. I'm going to grab a bite to eat here.

—I'll be there in two hours. He can't see you! The fact he can't see you says everything to me.

When your husband worries, he shouts. He shouts if you don't take a cab at night, you could get hurt. He shouts if you forget your umbrella, you could get wet. He shouts. Usually you ignore him. Often you laugh. He can't shout now. He's in the office. You both are silent on the phone. He sighs; his voice softens.

—What are they going to do with their kid? Watch—they'll lose their kid because they can't recognize its face.

You and your husband share a sad little laugh.

—I'll be here at the bar.

You hang up the phone and consume two plates of hors d'oeuvres. Ahi tuna on garlic toast. Cold cuts. Fried bits of seaweed and vegetables. A pint and a half of beer. You feel relaxed and have now started a conversation with a red-faced Dutch man who tells you he's a Mason. You try to remember something about the Masons other than that you've heard they're a secretive conservative group of white men. You remember your sister calling them fascists. She calls a good many people fascists. Unfortunately, she's usually correct. You wonder idly if the man beside you is a fascist, how many people in the club are fascists. You're not fazed, just curious. You order another beer.

—What charities does the club support, you ask.

All people like to discuss charitable concerns. Last week you interviewed a Macanese businessman who was rumored to have cooperated with the Japanese in WWII, a man who committed many crimes in the process of building his manufacturing empire. You talked to him about his efforts on behalf of the Chinese panda bear. Everyone has a cause.

—We do work for charity. Lots of charity. Of course, people don't always know it's us doing it, says the Mason, nodding solemnly. We're anonymous. Private charities.

—I see. Wonderful.

You realize you're getting good at talking to fascists, rich fascists, because of your job. You try to think of when the Masons started. Were they linked to the KKK? The National Rifle Association? Tories? Republicans? The National Front? What are they exactly? Friendly old white men? You used to joke with your husband about conspiracy theories but after your mail was opened, your computer had problems, and the phone started to click, you both quit laughing about it.

—We're low key. If you give money, it doesn't mean you have to advertise it, he says modestly.

—Oh no, you're so right. That's true charity. Anonymous. So can anyone join?

—Oh yes, even Muslims and Catholics. We'll be starting a women's branch.

You try to imagine a dark-skinned Muslim woman pledging allegiance to the Masons. What kind of woman would be a Mason? You think of asking him for membership information to see how he'd react, but decide against it.

An hour or so later you are pleasantly buzzed. The man across the bar, your husband's friend, suddenly strides over. He has spotted you, seen you.

—How's work going, he asks.

—Splendid!

You use vocabulary like 'splendid,' 'marvelous,' 'fantastic,' 'amazing,' and 'stunning' all day long no matter what you're talking about. You used to use other words, but your editor thought you had an attitude problem. The only issue is that you have to say them enthusiastically, which is difficult. You see the man's back molar on the left. It has a big gold filling.

—We're going on holiday to Sydney. Heading to Oz, he says, molar flashing.

—Marvelous!

The more you drink the easier it is to talk. The conversation is intolerably pleasant. When did he see you exactly? You look at him and give a little wave of your hand like you did earlier.

—Who's here? he says curiously.

He looks to see who you're waving at.

—Just you. Did you see me wave?

—Buzz-buzz, you say. We're like bees. Yellow skin and black hair, like, like, like bees, you say loudly. Buzz-buzz. Bzzzzzz.

You make sounds and start flapping your hands.

—Bzzzzz. Bzzzzzz.

You laugh too loudly.

—You can't see us, you say, laughing while swallowing big gulps of air.

You start to laugh so hard your stomach hurts. He doesn't know what to do. He's starting to get upset. You're not laughing at him, though, but you can't stop laughing long enough to tell him that you're laughing because your only other choice would be to yell, throw a drink across the bar or walk out. You will walk out, but before you do, you decide to order another beer. The way he looks at you, you know he thinks you're completely crazy. His eyes tell you he never saw you. He can't see you. He doesn't see people who look like you. You can't laugh anymore. You become quiet.

—I don't see you either, you say to him calmly.

He looks confused and then begins to speak. His voice becomes embarrassed and angry. You hear the denial. Yes, he knows what you are saying. He knows why you laughed. The protestations get stronger. You study his outline, his expressions, the way he holds himself. You listen to the rise of his voice carefully as if to memorize it all, because slowly in front of you he is fading. His words are drowned by the clink of glasses; the haze of tobacco rises and his presence recedes, swallowed by the dim amber light.

THE BODY POLITIC, 1982

"I am not your servile Oriental sex object!" I yelled through a megaphone. "We will not accept our position in an ignorant imperialistic construct! Capitalism equals colonialism and sexism!"

For seventeen years in Watertown, Wisconsin my existence as a Korean, American, Korean-American (hyphen; no hyphen), Asian, Asian-American (hyphen; no hyphen) and even Oriental, had been a source of unremarkable familiarity, but after entering university in New York, my ethnicity became my sole raison d'être. My parents greeted my political and intellectual awakening with confusion: *what else could you be?* They tolerated my identity politics as they believed that fraternizing with other Asian students would ensure the performance of filial piety's sacred rites modernly defined as pursuing a lucrative career in medicine (second choice, law) and marrying a Korean man from a good family.

I was a member of ASA-Asian Sisters for Action, but participated in the new tri-college offshoot AFCAC-Asian Feminists for Central American Change rally upon the suggestion of Donna Chong, ASA's president. She had told me I demonstrated potential as a political leader: "You have a loud voice. It's great for rallies."

Weekend pamphleteering, volunteering and organizing offered the potential of meeting a cool boyfriend, anyone "political or artistic," and the marching and sign waving burned calories. I built my biceps and lost five pounds in the first month of joining ASA, which I privately thought was a decent political payoff. The more activism took over my life, the further I drifted from my deli-owning parents' dreams of medical school, but then again, what did they understand about The Movement?

I pledged mind and body to the Revolution, and joined every Asian student organization on campus, with a few exceptions: Chinese Bible Study-CBS and Korean Christians for Hope-KCH. The former was Taiwanese only, specifically four students who knew each other from high school in Taiwan. Korean Christians for Hope, known for their excellent post Sunday service lunch—I attended twice under the premise of joining in order to satisfy a craving for oxtail soup and *kimchi*—were adamant that all members be Bible thumping, fire and brimstone screaming, Hallelujah jumping Christians. Despite a proclivity to tolerate such deviants in the name of good works, at that particular juncture, my self-described status as an Agnostic-Socialist-Taoist made even the most hopeful Korean Christian wince and grimace.

I was a card-carrying member of Korean Students Association-KSA, Mao's Red Guard Squadron-MRGS, and Asian Media Watch-AMW, which led boycotts against any item that carried an 'Oriental' label. AWG-Asian Women's Group, an organization dominated by overseas FOB-'fresh off the boat' students from Mainland China and Korea and a few Tokyo-pop Hello Kitty babes (armed with melon flavored gum to ward off bad breath) was apolitical, its primary focus food. AWG was the only group I mentioned to my parents. I chaired the Poster Committee for AWG bake sales.

"Maybe you'll finally learn to cook," said my mother approvingly. "Do you need me to send you another box of ramen?"

Donna's rousing battle calls to unchain ourselves from the sexist shackles of the beauty and fashion industries prompted a wardrobe overhaul and a medicine cabinet purge. I donned my nondescript black turtleneck and blue jeans with defiance and clarity. My single concession to capitalistic vanity was Dark n' Foxy brand black eyeliner No. 2 Cleopatra Kohl. Would anyone notice a trace of eyeliner?

I publicly applauded Donna's talks on the hegemony of white beauty standards, but balked when she advocated that all ASA members cut their hair. She got a crew cut; it looked terrible.

"Hollywood images have led people to associate long-haired Asian women as bar girls. Long hair is a racial stereotype," said Donna solemnly gazing at my waist-length hair.

I'm not cutting it. Donna can fuck off. Rebelling from Rebellion? I had neither the desire, nor the will, to break away from Asian Sisters for Action. I had waist-length hair since I was eight years old, and its length and luster was the object of envy and admiration. After a few weeks of anguish, I walked into an East Village hair salon and sold it for fifty dollars. I slouched over to a pink padded chair where my tresses were snipped to a liberated two-inch length and sobbed as soon as I left the shop. The next day I bought a black beret off a street vendor.

At the ASA meeting a week later, the agenda of Thai and Filipino sex tourism was usurped by the ins and outs of my breezy, layered, up-to-the-minute haircut. Feigning boredom with the flattery, I said, "I feel free. Who needs all that hair?" Donna nodded her approval, but later pulled me aside.

"You had beautiful hair. It wasn't a stereotype. I mean, it was just a speech. I hate my short hair," she admitted.

"I didn't need all of that hair. I feel released," I said casually twisting the strands.

I tried my best to embody the ideals of progress, and change. My unflagging enthusiasm did not go unnoticed by the top brass Chinese and Korean American pre-law senior males at the nascence of their long and arduous ascent as corporate tax attorneys for Fortune 500 companies, yet I was soon informed that I exhibited inappropriate or 'counterrevolutionary' behavior, inconsistencies which could and should be swiftly amended in order to better 'move our people forward.'

"Your miniskirt is small," emphasized Sam Choi-KSA president.

"Small?"

"Short," he said seriously. "It's okay, though."

"What's that supposed to mean?"

"Not a lot of Korean freshman girls, er, 'women' wear clothes like you do," he said.

My skirts were short. I wore fishnet stockings. Guys stared. I liked it, although I wasn't supposed to, especially if it was a white male. *What about the nice blond guy who walks with me everyday to art history class from the student cafe? Traitor! What about the black guy in my biology lab? It's better to disavow stereotyping.*

*   *   *

A few months later I found myself sipping a beer at a Park Avenue penthouse fundraiser for a Tibetan orphanage. The hosts were a glamorous tall Mandarin-speaking man with a chestnut beard and a raw silk shirt and his petite Chinese Malaysian wife bedecked in jade and Balinese batik. Their exotic apartment was filled with antique medicine chests and brass gongs, Turkish silk carpets and Vietnamese watercolor paintings. Sandalwood incense burned in the corner and made my nose hairs tingle. I fingered a brocade table runner while admiring a pyramid of gloriously smooth tangerines and clasped my hands to stop my palms and fingers from touching everything in sight. I had entered a photo layout from a design magazine and walked slowly around the living room, mesmerized by perfectly positioned objects, and the chic manners and dress of people who had traveled the world.

The Swensens were the only mixed couple I knew in Wisconsin. Mrs. Swensen faithfully attended Korean church service and was married to a former GI who owned the downtown hardware store. Like most of the Koreans in Watertown, their home was decorated with furniture from Sears, their floors were linoleum blue, and in their living room was a small black lacquer chest inlaid with mother-of-pearl almost identical to my mother's.

After a brief lecture on the Dalai Lama, the party grew louder, and I found myself face-to-face with sloe-eyed Martin, a dark-haired man in his late twenties clad in a black leather motorcycle jacket. He offered me a beer and within minutes our lips were inches apart. He told me my beret made me the ideal gamine, and when I took it off, complimented my hairstyle and carefully touched the short wisps. Our bodies slid towards each other, and I enjoyed the rush in my stomach as he stroked my cheeks. His fingers ran up my spine.

"You have beautiful lips," Martin said kissing me. He quickly guided me to the bedroom where people had stored their coats and jackets and we swiftly embraced, wrapped in the smell of clove cigarettes and the taste of beer. Our hands fumbled and groped each other's flesh through our clothing. He reached up my shirt and pulled me closer before I abruptly turned away, rejecting his casual offer to accompany him home. I was in control. I sauntered back into the party, prompting Martin to follow me out of the bedroom and watch me catwalk over to the bar as I tossed my non-existent hair, and loudly chatted to a few friends. He smiled and I coolly looked away. I felt in control; I wanted a man to possess feelings of unstoppable and irrational passion for me.

Martin wanted to fuck.

Martin had lived a life outside of university. He was the embodiment of an image I held in my mind of the quintessential New York intellectual: hardened despite his relative youth, raw in energy and demeanor, with a stare that suggested danger, if only in my imagination. With his dark hair, moonlight skin and razor stubble, fully clad in black and wearing glasses which carefully perched at the end of his nose, making his deep liquid eyes appear all the more deadly and vulnerable, he impressed me with his soliloquy on third world women and the exploitation of the lower classes. He quoted Karl Marx and Laozi and was friends with a Nicaraguan filmmaker who had been shot in the leg. Martin was an authentic student revolutionary, a breed familiar to me only through books and journals that reported political activities overseas. He was exactly the kind of man I had envisioned as my destiny, a rebel who would cement my arrival as a revolutionary, woman, and sophisticate. In between groping and fumbling, he had managed to convey the story of his young event-packed life: after dropping out of university, a stint in the Navy—during which time he became a pacifist and studied Zen Buddhism—he traveled around the world for a few years and now was back at university studying filmmaking and working as a bartender. Earlier that fall, I had enrolled in 1930's Socialist Musical Film of the Soviet Union, but I dropped after falling asleep during the first lecture. I was glad I didn't mention it to Martin; he told me his friend was the instructor.

Before college I had escaped to the darkened theaters to watch the Hollywood factory images of beautiful women and men erupt into a volcanic climax of passionate kissing. Since then, my cinematic diet had been reduced to ascetic fare: documentaries on refugees, nuclear waste, and the occasional subtitled film. The grainier the footage, the more wobbly the camera angles, the more obscure the subject, the better the film, or so I tried to convince myself: film of and for the people.

I was intrigued by Martin's aspirations, yet vowed to dedicate my own future to more weighty matters: discriminatory legislation, the greenhouse effect, and the proliferation of corporate America. I had never pondered making movies other than the time the newspaper announced an open casting call for a movie based on the story of *Heidi*. I sent in my picture like every other ten-year-old girl in the United States. My mother laughed, but didn't stop me.

"You might be a strange-looking Heidi," said Mom, braiding my hair. I handed her the Polaroid camera.

"I don't care. Why can't I be Heidi?"

"Koreans aren't actresses. You should be a doctor."

"I don't want to be a doctor. I want to be an actress."

"Okay, smile, Heidi. I'll take the picture. Hurry."

"*Kimchi*," I said giving my best Alps smile and cocking my head like Heidi did in my picture book.

"Swiss don't eat *kimchi*. I think you'd better say *fondue*," said Mom.

"What's *fondue*?" Later that year I tried fondue at my school's International Food Fair. I loved Heidi's food. For my birthday, Mom borrowed a fondue pot with six skewers from Mrs. Swensen, and I dipped white-tipped strawberries and sugary canned pineapple into a warm melted chocolate wearing my new baby blue nightgown with white lace trim.

✳   ✳   ✳

Martin and I had exchanged numbers at the party, but I found myself waiting by the phone. *Feminists don't wait for phone calls. They make them.* I couldn't. What would I say to him? Normally loquacious, at the party I was in awe, held captive by his stories, silenced by the scope of his experience. He called two days later.

"How are you, Sabrina?" asked Martin over the phone in his sleepy slurred whisper. The timbre of his voice sounded as if he had awoken from a nap necessitated by a late-night drunken stupor. Slow. Hushed. Raspy. Sexy.

"I'm fine."

"Would you like to come over for tea?" he asked.

"For tea?" I imagined the Brontes and heard the clattering of thin white china edged with yellow roses. I envisioned my desperate run out on the moors in a velvet dress and dirty leather shoes with little buttons, chasing a pneumonia-racked man in flounced sleeves, before collapsing with a fever to await my bleeding by leeches. I'd never been asked to tea. "Okay. When?"

"What are you doing now?"

"Nothing. Actually, I'm busy. I'm reading uhm, Ghandi," I said looking at a book's smooth spine.

"Great. We can talk non-violent protest when you come over. Cross over on 106th. Go down Amsterdam, but get over to the east side of the street once you hit 105th. The corner building with the blue door sells drugs, so try to watch it."

"Oh."

"I'll walk down to meet you at the door in exactly one hour," said Martin.

I changed my clothes twice and put on my lavender bra and matching bikini underwear. I wasn't sure what it was that the Asian Sisters would inevitably dislike about Martin, but I guessed it was the qualities about him that I too, thought unfamiliar. Unknowable. Exotic. Peculiar. *Caucasian.*

Asian Sisters dated, I reminded myself, especially Donna, although she had been steady with Sam Choi for several weeks. Eligible Sam was regularly trailed by throngs of AWG members offering to do his laundry. "It's such a drag. We gotta free ourselves of the patriarchy," said Sam.

Rumor had it that Donna had told Sam to wash his own "goddamn fucking underwear you loser," which had only furthered Sam's desire for Donna. Rumor also had it that after Kathy Kim broke up with her, Donna freely gave blow jobs, or so said Matt Matsumoto, who went on a date with Donna before Sam. Feminists, bi-feminists in particular, were girlfriend material. Feminists didn't do laundry, but gave head and didn't expect monogamy. Not a bad deal, KSA guys agreed. Asian Women's Group-AWG did laundry and cooked, but Asian Sisters for Action-ASA put out.

I went down Broadway, air clean from a recent cold rain, the color in the streets popping bright as a board game, red apples piled high in bins as red electric as the stoplights and the pouts of the students heading back to campus. I cut over on 106th street, kicking a plastic bag as a bus moved down the block like a slow hippopotamus, groaning and farting black air. I hit Amsterdam and turned right. The dollar store's windows burst with scrawled sign advertisements: two-for-one deals, dishwashing detergent, children's socks, and carpet remnants. Dusk cut through the air, chopping it thin and cool. People ducked indoors for TV warmth. A few steps from the blue door I heard a bellowing cry, the scramble of feet and fists, and the rumble of arguing men. A scuffle broke out and a bottle crashed onto the ground scattering jagged glass like chipped ice. I banged on Martin's door and called up to his window, giving a tremendous kick to the solid wood door as he bounded down the stairs.

"Hello, Sabrina. You look flushed and lovely," he said smiling.

"I think there's something with the blue door. Nothing I'm sure," I said in a halting voice.

"Wrong. It's something, just not anything new," said Martin. "Don't hold the rail. Splinters," he said, shutting the front door behind me. The hallway had peeling paint and a row of rusted mailboxes. A baby cried and the stairs wheezed under the weight of our feet.

The small apartment was in disarray. I peeked into his bedroom. There was a desk with stacks of papers, mounds of clothes on the floor, and a loft bed. A tape recorder in the living room played a scratchy Elvis Costello tune while I nervously sat on his lumpy sofa. A huge poster of an Italian movie covered the wall. *A starving New York filmmaker. How cool.* I glanced at my reflection in the mirror and brushed my hair over a blemish blooming in the center of my forehead.

"Sit down. Want a massage?" asked Martin, stroking my neck. He threw my coat on a wobbly stuffed chair covered with a tapestry of elephants and dug his thumbs and fingers into my lower back.

"Ouch," I said.

"*Shiatsu*," said Martin.

"What's that?"

"Japanese massage."

"I'm not Japanese."

"You don't have to be to enjoy a *shiatsu* massage. Nice back," said Martin.

"Do you have tea?" I asked, moving away. Martin's fingers jabbed like sticks.

"Sure. Tea for the lovely mademoiselle," he said, heading to the kitchen. I kicked off my shoes and studied the titles crammed on his shelves. In the corner were postcards from Europe, reels of film, and a dented 16 mm movie projector atop a rickety metal cart.

"You show movies here?" I called out to the kitchen.

"When I have the right company."

"Who's Marquis de Sade?" I opened a book featuring photos of black and white bodies in various sexual poses. *To Martin/My heart and dungeon, my heaven and hell/Lover, master, servant and desire/Rosemary.* My old boyfriend Christos, my high school's exchange student from Greece, had presented me a picture book on Athens. *To Sabrina/One day I hope you can visit my country/Love Christos.*

"Read it." He set two mugs of steaming tea on a milk crate. "These are hot. Better wait."

I imagined Rosemary as Martin's exotic lover—the multilingual printmaker with a narrow jaw and high cheekbones who favored sex in yoga positions against the wall. Christos and I had sex three times total and my artistic endeavors were limited to designing posters for the AWG bake sale. My face was round like a moon; I spoke no Korean; I knew one phrase in French: *Croque Madame s'il vous plait.*

"I don't like Nietzsche," I said, touching a frayed paperback on the floor, trying to remember details of my high school honors philosophy seminar. "I really don't consider myself an existentialist in the traditionally defined sense. Too bleak."

"'Bleak,' well that's a description," he chuckled.

"Of course, Nietzsche's philosophy doesn't really work when thinking about sexism or racism. Discrimination, you know."

"Oh?" Martin's interest was piqued.

"Lotus flower stuff, that white male-Asian female hang-up," I said, thinking to myself that I was repeating what Martin already knew, the speech Donna delivered to new members of ASA about structures and empowerment.

"Interesting," said Martin.

"You like movies, I guess." On top of the television were books on film theory, cinematographers, directors and set design. I felt cautious; not enough curiosity and he would think I wasn't interested, too much and he would know the depth of my ignorance and laugh at my naiveté.

"Don't you?"

"Yeah, I do. Ouch, kind of burned my tongue," I giggled.

Martin took the mug from me. "Let's kiss it," he said grabbing me. I saw his tongue sticking out and I shut my eyes, oddly stimulated, chilled, wanting the warmth from his body. He impatiently unbuttoned my shirt and tossed it on the ground, then unsnapped my bra, but despite the heat of arousal, when he tried to unzip my jeans I moved away.

"Oh, Christ, now what? What are you doing?" he said exasperated.

"Nothing. I have an itch."

"Should I scratch it?"

"No, it's fine. I'm cold," I said, picking up my bra and stuffing it in my jeans. I put on my shirt and swiftly buttoned it the wrong way.

I wasn't sure if I wanted to kiss Martin anymore; I wanted to go back to my dorm room and take a shower. I felt goose bumps rising on my upper arms, my breasts shrinking from the cool air, my nipples hard and small. Stiff toes. I regretted wearing old socks. There was a tiny hole in the left heel that I did not want Martin to see; the exposed skin was dry and the stray threads of the sock snagged on the sharp splinters of his uneven wood floor. I stayed because if I left it would expose my apprehension and then Martin the revolutionary, the man who had traveled the world, would not be the slightest bit interested in Sabrina the deli owner's daughter, former church choir soprano, undeclared major from Wisconsin.

"Do you want anything to eat?" asked Martin.

"Maybe."

"I think I have something to munch on," he said, heading to the kitchen. He slammed a few cabinet doors and brought out an opened bag of Oreo cookies.

"Cookies?"

"No thanks. Well, I'll have one." We munched and chatted and when the cookies were done, Martin folded the bag into a narrow funnel, inhaled the last of the crumbs and threw the plastic bag on the floor.

"Enough of this stuff. Why don't you get a little more comfortable," said Martin smoothly pinching the flesh of my exposed stomach. I kissed him back as his tongue slid over my teeth and my lipstick smeared the corners of his crumb-covered mouth. He nimbly unbuttoned my shirt for the second time, but when he again tried to unzip my pants, I sat upright on the sofa and awkwardly buttoned my shirt. I picked up a book about silent movies and tried to remember if I'd read something about how to behave with Martin. I couldn't think of anything.

"Tea," I said. I sipped tea as he began to kiss my neck. "Wait a second," I said, scratching my neck.

Martin spoke quietly and we began to kiss again, but when I straightened my posture and clothes, and pushed his hands away from my jeans, he let out an impatient snort and angrily sputtered, "Don't pull this crap on me. Do I have to treat you like a little China dolly? All women expect this bullshit." He ambled over to his bookshelf and lit a cigarette while I squirmed.

"No, it's not that," I said swallowing. My mouth was dry, saliva spent.

"Don't be a child. Just relax," ordered Martin. He sat back down and pressed up against my flesh, covering my body with his.

His blatant desire pulled me out of my cave. I stiffened and then let my body go strangely limp and fall dead into his, fall away, fall in, bury deep, bury down. I responded and then stopped. I left my body and watched. An ambivalent surrender. A live thing. A dead thing. He took off my clothing piece-by-piece and I shut my eyes and heard the buzz from a drill, tires ripping against the road, and the whir of the fruit market's overhead fan. He hovered; I blinked and held my breath and his touch cut paper sharp. I felt the heaviness of my body pushing my feet to the floor and the slowing of my blood, and sucked out his bitter center, licking for the absent syrup.

Do you have to like the person you sleep with? Martin made me feel a little sexy, but a little frightened and I dropped myself into him with loathing and unknowing. *If I really wanted to, it would stop, right?* Martin prodded me to the bedroom, his hand like a stick against my flanks. I couldn't get my body to move.

"What are you doing? Let's go into the other room." I looked at Martin; his eyes softened. "Come on Sabrina, it's nicer in the bedroom. You'll like it."

I hesitated, but stepped inside the small bedroom. *This was not what sex was supposed to be, right?* I stood before his loft bed and began to climb, the bottom of my bare foot pressed against the first rung of the ladder. I looked down at the chipped purple nail polish on my big toe. The angry eyes, his curled lips—I did not want to go up the ladder, but obeyed—the voice commanding, the voice certain, the voice suffocating my own. I stepped onto the ladder's second rung and then paused. My voice and limbs were silent and torn: mute, amputated, cut out. He turned me to face the ladder and I robotically climbed. I tripped on the last step, but Martin caught me before I fell and ushered me up to the bed.

The tiny loft bed was positioned so that the head and the foot of the bed were snug against two walls and one side of the bed was pushed against the room's only window. Martin's horizontal body blocked me in, a barricade in front of the ladder facing the bedroom door. A dirty gray mattress without sheets and two musty pillows with faded pillowcases were bunched up in a corner. To my right was a frosted window with bars to fend off intruders; to my left was Martin crawling all over my flesh.

I looked up and thought of how the swirled pattern of the ceiling made the shape of a fat three-legged raccoon. On the ceiling the raccoon ran up the side of a tall dark tree and disappeared into midnight. Fade in. The end. My eyes returned to the permanent dust covering a ceiling that would never fall. Martin handed me a box.

"What is it?" I asked hesitantly.

"Here, you put it inside of you. It's foam. Birth control."

"I've never used it."

"It works like a tampon." He took out a long slender plastic white tube from the light blue box. I fumbled to insert the foam between my legs.

Martin threw the box on the floor and lifted himself on top of me as I lay long and wooden, my pores shrieking as he furiously heaved. I wanted to howl, pierce the dark, but all that came out was a baby hiccup. I held my breath, my jaw taut and rigid as my heart readied to explode. The dry walls between my legs felt the hammering of raw flesh against flesh. I let myself record the moment—*this will all be irrelevant later*—I pictured myself popping ahead, careening in an unknown tunnel, the near and far bending as the dimensions intersected in a black hole. I pushed my body up to the sky, breathing out of my mouth to shut out his smell. I was exposed, but longed to burrow into the bed's quicksand spots, escape by suffocating in the mattress stuffing.

It lasted but a few moments. In my mind, I was yelling, kicking, and pummeling him with my fists, throwing his belongings into a bonfire in the middle of the apartment. In an angry tornado I pushed his body into the blaze while his anguished cries filled the room and I ran out the door. This picture melted frame by frame, a reel of gray-brown blotches: a paramecium, an amoeba, stretched against an iceberg-white screen. In truth, I was petrified, an icy corpse pulled from a deep lake. Martin gave one final shove and grunt, finishing the act with the barest acknowledgement of the body beneath him. My eyes welled when I saw the blood. I turned away.

"Sorry, I came so fast. Shit, are you a virgin?" asked Martin with surprise looking at the blood.

"No."

He came back from the bathroom with a dirty white towel and blotted the blood between my legs leaving a pale-pink smear on my inner thigh.

"I'm fine." I thought about Christos saying he loved me and both of us crying at the airport when he left for Greece. He sent a postcard before I left for college. He didn't ask me to visit. I never wrote back. "Do you remember who you lost your virginity to?"

"A girl in France. Long time ago."

"Were you in love?"

"I suppose."

"I was in love," I blurted.

"You don't always have to be in love with the people you have sex with. Sex is great because of the conversations you have afterwards," said Martin quietly.

I had nothing to say.

"You should experience as much as you can. At university there are thousands of sexually eligible men and women. Never at another point in your life will it be this way."

"I want to go home now." I turned away to look out the window, but it was dark. On the other side of the glass was the blue door, the street with stores filled of tins of biscuits and cookies, dishwashing liquid and toothpaste piled in large plastic bins. I could taste warm mango juice. A nut-sized lump hardened in my throat. I wanted to gag. "I have to go to the bathroom, please." He moved and I climbed down the ladder. I dressed and blankly stared at the books scattered around his apartment. Martin insisted on escorting me to dinner.

At the Hunan Plate restaurant, a layer of film coated the plates of limp broccoli drenched in too much soy sauce and cheap stale oil.

"Why aren't you eating?" said Martin wolfing down his food.

"I'm dieting."

"You don't need to diet. You look fine."

"I'm not hungry," I said stubbornly. I took a few bites of rice. Long grain. Light and thin. Slender. Fluffy. I remembered the first time I ate long grain rice.

"What's wrong with this rice, Mom?" I asked her.

"What do you mean?"

"Why doesn't it stick? It's not sticking. Did they cook this right?"

"It's long grain rice. Chinese eat long grain. Koreans eat short grain," said Mom.

"I like short grain. This falls off my chopsticks," I said. Martin's chopsticks were perfectly straight—impeccable technique—he deftly picked up morsels of food and politely excused himself when he gave a small burp. My chopsticks remained crossed like a child's.

Martin grabbed my plate, ravenously ate the broccoli and tore at the beef, taking big bites with his orthodontic-straight teeth, white and even as a movie star's. Grease from the noodles stuck to the corners of his mouth as he slurped the tea and finished off the rice. A piece of broccoli stuck between his bottom teeth.

"I just don't feel well," I said.

"Drink your tea then," ordered Martin. I sipped on my lukewarm tea and pretended to study an overweight woman snap beans onto the newspaper in the corner of the restaurant. I remembered snapping beans for the KSA-Korean Students Association dinner and laughing with Donna. She said she was trying not to fall in love with Sam because he was exactly what her family would want, but that she was falling in love with him anyway, and he had said the same thing to her.

We parted on the corner. Martin kissed me good-bye on my cheek and as soon as he turned around, I ran harder than I ever had in my life. I was sweating and panting by the time I reached the front entrance of my building, my armpits damp and collar wet, my shirt sticking to my back. I gave a nod to the security guard at the desk, sprinted up ten flights of stairs, leapt into the shower and spit out the taste of him and grease. I scrubbed my skin until it was pink, barely toweling off the water. I shut off the lights, crawled into bed, put my head on a pillow and pretended to kiss Christos. I was sore between my legs for two days.

A few weeks later I was voted vice president of AWG-Asian Women's Group and was asked out by Matt Matsumoto. For some reason, I wondered if I should mention Martin to him, a desire to confide, to confess an error, a mistake. A past. I had one now, though I wasn't sure what kind. But I kept my silence after the AMW-Asian Media Watch meeting. Sam spoke of Asian sisters who sold out their people to white men and I could feel Matt squeeze my hand as I disappeared in his palm. I wasn't a sellout, he was saying to me. Not long after, I used my failing grade in biology to break up with Matt, telling him that my parents were expecting me to go to medical school and I needed to study more. Donna said that Matt would be there for me after I passed my final exam in biology. I didn't tell her that I wasn't sure if I would be there for him, or for anyone or anything else.

After flunking my biology exam, I learned that Donna dumped Sam for Matt. I told Donna our friendship was more important than a guy, but used the complication to resign from the vice-presidency of AWG-Asian Women's Group.

"Leaders are not born, they're made," said Donna hoping to appeal to my sense of duty.

"I'm not sure what I want to be made into," I said.

I saw Martin once after that day in his apartment. By then I had left my parents' dream of medical school behind in favor of poetry and theater, my hair was long enough to tie back in a neat ponytail, and I had dropped my membership to AWG after their polite, but distant response to my new boyfriend Malcolm, whom I had met in biology lab. Malcolm was black, allergic to alcohol, and an aspiring engineer with thick glasses. He played the viola and showed me how to cha-cha. Our presence as a couple that could not claim membership to one group seemed to raise questions of loyalty from all sides: black and yellow. Neither one of us wanted to defend or explain, so we negotiated a space that skimmed both groups without belonging to either.

I had tried to forget about Martin, but a year later he was crossing the street and greeted me like an old friend, asking for my phone number. I felt embarrassed seeing him and for no other reason than my wish to pretend that nothing had happened, I scrawled my name on the matchbook he handed me. As soon as I did, I regretted my actions and hoped that he would never call. He never did.

For a long time, I viewed Martin as my first introduction to casual sex and sexual politics. I didn't know how else to explain him to myself, and maybe too, it was that I was afraid to acknowledge what had happened. In memory he existed in that murky domain between consent and refusal, anger and indifference, naiveté and corruption. As an adolescent, I could not see the schism between action and words, and my sorrow only came years later when I realized how easy it is for innocence to be lost in the brutal quest for understanding and self. It was only then that I understood that what I had wanted to become at that time was nothing more than the body I had been all along, that humanity is fragile, people are contradictory, and politics are always personal.

CANYON

It's not easy to become American. When I arrived in the U.S., I went to high school for two long years. The first year, my clothes weren't like the ones other girls wore so they punched and slapped me, ripped my shirt and said it didn't look right with my skirt and laughed and snapped the elastic of my bra against my back. They pulled at the corners of their eyes and called me Crazy Chink—following me down the halls when the teachers weren't looking, stepping on my heels and kicking at my calves. When I told my aunt, my mother's cousin, she told me I had to ignore them, that they weren't going to amount to anything. But it was hard to do. Every day I cried in the bathroom at school.

It took a while to learn English. The English teacher spoke to our class in Spanish to teach us English and when I tried to explain this to my aunt, all she said was that I had better learn English fast if I was going to make my family proud. What good was learning Spanish if I wanted to be American? A girl named Anna helped me with my Spanish and English and we became friends, her clothes looking only slightly better than mine, and so I was able to graduate, but by then my aunt told me I needed to do more to earn my keep. Right after graduation I started working full-time at the Pretty Nails salon in Koreatown.

Work has helped my English. This fall, I'm taking English classes for my associate degree. I tell Young one day my children will be at the top of their class. Young says his children will be doctors, lawyers, or computer experts. He wants money; his fantasy is to wade through a field of dollars, full glorious blooms, the flower of America. Although he works doing deliveries, Young dreams of a nice house, a fast car, and expensive clothes. He says the U.S. has infinite possibilities.

Together we stand ready to jump, yet we always back off. We're both careful, but there is no one else I can imagine marrying. I feel myself easing into his body, promising to be wonderful and flooding the deep corners of his heart. I didn't realize how lonely I was before we met. I sometimes find myself erecting fences, digging holes, and nailing pieces of careful behavior into place as obstacles. But Young is patient. He is five years older than I am, handsome and lean with dark brown eyes and a cute boyish face. I tell him he could have a girlfriend much prettier than myself. I told him this as we walked down the Bright Angel Trail at the Grand Canyon.

"Oh yes, who would I rather have?" he said pinching my waist.

"Others," I insisted.

"You know what I like about you?" he teased.

"What?"

"You tell me what you think," said Young.

"That's not so easy."

"Tell me about it. But I'd rather be with someone who tells the truth. If I wanted to be with someone who agreed with me all of the time, then I certainly wouldn't be with you," he said laughing.

Sometimes I'm so excited to see him that I have no control. I run up to him and chatter, talking his ears off as he laughs and laughs. Other times, we sit and hold hands in silence. He tells me, "Hana, life is hard but you don't have to be. Don't worry so much." Young makes things seem possible.

We had arrived at Bright Angel Trail as the sun came up, an egg yolk spilling out over the rugged green and rust-colored sloping dirt walls. As cool air ran up my back, I grabbed Young from behind and bounced up and down, almost knocking him over as we faced each other for a kiss. From where I stood, it looked just like it did in the pictures, tall dark trees poised against jagged rocks, mosaic patterns weaving in and out, and winding paths dotted with small islands of trees and brush splashing into the blue-blue sky. We came to the Grand Canyon because Young said that since the U.S. is our country now, it's important to see its famous sites.

"It's amazing. The United States is so big," said Young. "In every way."

"I can walk forever," I said.

"It's nice that we're here so early," said Young.

He was about to say we were alone, but as we turned the corner, a woman dressed in a wrinkled red dress and black street shoes appeared further down the path carrying two plastic grocery store bags. The faded bags bulged, the name of the store emblazoned on the sides in bright orange.

She sat down on a rock for a moment to rest halfway down the path to the bottom. Middle-aged with dark hair and cinnamon-colored skin, she was striding purposefully, limbs close to her side, calm and even in her steps. As she walked, her bodily ease told her secret, no faltering in her step, no stumbling on the path. Sure-footed like a doe, she seemed to know where to skip and pause, where to jump over the cracks, which stones were easily overturned, and the exact time of day to stare at the walls to make out faces and maps, battles and animals. When I saw her I almost wondered if she was real. There was nothing to separate her from the light and dark of the land. I felt awkward after looking at her. Wearing my light blue shoes and bright pink top, nothing about me belonged to the Canyon.

I'll always be a stranger here; I always feel eyes on my face and shoulders, but I can make a home in the United States. A shamed family and a lost child, what did I have in Korea? I have money in the bank. I have Young. I speak English and I drive an eight-year-old Toyota car that has one side that does not look very nice, but a fine engine. A customer offered it to me, and I got a good price.

Young was right. It was a smart purchase. Before I had to take the bus everywhere. It made life impossible. With a car, I'm free. I've driven all over the city and to the beach on Sundays. One weekend, we went on an overnight trip to Palm Springs. I tried golfing, which Young enjoyed, but I found rather boring. When no one is with me, I speed, bravely flying up the freeway, looking out and seeing the blue green water and for a moment, I am living my American dream; anything is possible.

In those moments, I sense that my child is fine, and that he is happy with another family, in another city, in another place. I think he must have a mother who puts a cap on his head when it rains and who watches him walk and stumble and look out a window. I feel peculiarly relieved; my burden blows away, and I can forget about him for a little while.

I cut out pictures of places I'd like to visit. The first picture I taped on my door was an aerial view of the Grand Canyon. As the assistant manager of the Pretty Nails salon, I am on familiar terms with quite a few customers. I can read people well, or so Soo tells me, and it pays off. I'm always tipped well.

I was so excited after my first ride to the beach that I gave Nancy a free bikini wax. She comes in twice a month and I've showed her how to shape her eyebrows. Her eyebrows look like a man's and she has coarse hair and big eyes, a long pointed nose and flower-petal lips like the models in fashion magazines. I've seen her dressed on TV in a safari outfit holding cologne. We chat together in Spanish and English and when she leaves she always gives me a kiss and a hug. I find her pretty in her large and masculine way, although I admit when she first flexed the muscles in her arms and legs I thought she looked like a bodybuilder or wrestler. I know now, I was just being old-fashioned.

These days everyone at the salon wants to be more muscular and some of the girls have joined a gym. I joined after Young suggested it and he showed me how to work the weight machines. Small weights. Lots of repetition. That way you don't get too many muscles. I guess everyone wants to be bigger. In Korea, they too admire the exaggerated and the big, although not in women. Big cars, big homes, big voices. Size means plenty, and plenty is the U.S.A., and the U.S.A. means money. Nancy's laugh sounds like that merry American laugh; the easy laugh that comes from a huge house and a shiny large car and plenty of everything: soft silk clothes, perfumed bars of pastel soap, and glittering rings of silver and gold. Occasionally she gives me things, like magazines or furniture.

"I'm getting rid of a lamp. Do you want it?" asked Nancy.

"A lamp?"

"For reading, on a desk. Small lamp. Just cleaning out the house." She is always throwing things away.

"I don't need it, but thank you," I said politely.

"I have no use for it," she insisted.

"No, thank you."

"Are you sure? It is a very nice lamp. I don't want to throw it away. I'd rather have someone I know take it. Please take it. Please. It would be doing me a great favor," Nancy smiled.

"Lamp?"

"Yes. Otherwise, I'll just throw it away. I don't want to do that."

"Thank you, but it's not necessary. I don't need anything," I protested.

"Hana, please. I insist. Please."

"Okay."

"Good. I'll bring it in the next time. If you really don't want it and don't like it, then give it to another girl. But I think you'll like it," she said.

Her throwaways are sent to furnish my life. We go through the ritual every time. It's only polite. I too, toss things aside, but only after they are so crumpled and faded they have no other purpose. My dress turns into a shirt or a smock, then a rag for polishing a shelf, then the floor, then my shoes. Buttons are clipped off and saved in a small box. Tinfoil is washed and stacked in little plastic containers. I save key chains, small snippets of colored ribbon, free pens and maps, and jars of every size and shape.

Amongst Nancy's first discards were several stacks of *National Geographic* magazines. I spent hours looking at the photographs of orange frogs and dinosaur bones and telescopic views of planets. I was talking to Young of stars and the galaxy and so for my twenty-first birthday we went to the planetarium to look at the black crystal-filled sky. He squeezed my knee and traced my palm with his fingers. Under the dome, the universe was safe, under the dome, the darkness did not swallow, under the dome, the deep midnight viewed from a brown plush chair was a rich baritone singing into our hearts.

"What happens to us?" I worriedly asked Young.

"We're going to get ice cream," he assured me.

"No, no, afterwards. Death. The sky."

"We'll go to heaven. At least that's where I am going; I hope," he joked. "I don't know about you…And we'll be happy, up there. In heaven, with God."

Young is always so certain about these kinds of things. He prides himself on his ability to find his way in any situation. When we pulled up to the Canyon Motel he declared that we didn't have to look at any other motel. I was about to argue with him, who takes the first motel room they see? But when we walked into the room, I saw he was right. Twenty-three dollars a night. The bed was clean and the small bar of white soap was wrapped in orange paper with a pine tree design. I had a craving for soup and directly across the street was a restaurant that had my favorite—New England clam chowder. Young speaks plainly and thoughtfully, no matter my questions. With Young I feel independent, yet truthfully he rarely is more than a few words away.

Young climbed on top of a big boulder and I scrambled up next to him. "This is made by God. Look at this view, and you know you're in his presence."

"I don't believe," I mumbled.

"I know that, Hana. I know everyone has their own belief," he said, massaging my shoulder. He paused to look at my expression, waiting for me to agree. I didn't say anything and peered at the canyon walls hoping to see a familiar shape.

"I'm telling you what I think."

"Yes," said Young glumly. "It's just difficult." He gave my hand a squeeze and I tried to smile.

"It is," I agreed.

"Why did you frown?"

"Nothing," I said, looking away. "Where are you going?"

"To take photos," he said curtly. He bought an expensive telephoto lens to bring to the canyon for pictures of small flowers and plants, tiny things we never have time to see. Young is camera crazy. We take a picture almost every weekend. On our first date we took a picture in a photo booth at the mall. It was the first time I had my picture taken with a man.

Young pursued me. He would stop by the salon and pretend to talk to Soo and try to flirt with me. I was friendly, and kept my distance, but he gradually began to wear me down. When he heard I was going to share an apartment with Soo, he offered to help move the chest of drawers Nancy had given me. My aunt's apartment was crowded with new relatives and she was expecting a new baby.

"It's too heavy," I said.

"Why do you think I'm offering to move it?" said Young.

"No, it's too much trouble for you."

"How are you going to move the chest of drawers?"

"I can manage," I said stubbornly.

"Hana, it's not a problem," said Young. "The real problem will be if you keep saying no, because then we will waste away the day and nothing will get done." Young loves teasing me. That day we had so much fun together. That day I laughed so hard I almost cried.

I tried to touch Young's shoulder. He took a step sideways. I closed my eyes and could feel him running fast and long, tasting the sweat from his pores, as my thighs burned and calves ached. I could not keep up—I nearly fell. He was sprinting: a whirr, a blur, a ghost. I opened my eyes to find him in the same place and watched as he stooped to pick up a rock and throw it hard against a tree. A piece of the tree's bark chipped off and the rock fell to the ground with a loud thud.

"You're upset."

"No."

"I can become a Christian," I whispered. "I'm sorry."

"That's not the point. If you don't believe, you don't believe. Faith should be real," said Young.

"I don't really see the problem if we believe differently," I said finally.

"It is a problem," he said in a clipped voice. "How can we be together if we don't believe in the same thing?" We go to church together now and have agreed our children would be Christians. Young has said our disagreement was not important, people change.

He waits and I see his clear eyes and I think: if I become a Christian does it erase what came before? Although I have wrapped my arms around him, felt his lips on my cheeks and the rhythm of his promises and pleasure in the dark, I have stayed quiet. I have tasted his skin, his hands have run smoothly down my legs and up my body, and the light touch of his fingers on my breasts have said everything to me, yet I remain silent.

*   *   *

"Anything you cannot bring, don't worry, you can buy it in California," said my mother. She watched as I packed my shoes, carefully wrapping them in plastic bags before stuffing them inside the green vinyl suitcase with the broken handle.

"Here's some money," she said handing me bills in an envelope.

"Thank you." I turned away and pretended to sneeze so she could not see me wipe my eyes.

"I saved it for an emergency like this. Be a good girl. Your relatives say that California is a very nice place."

*   *   *

That was the last time we spoke in person. I call once a month.

When I first came to this country, I worked hard and didn't do anything but watch TV, go to school and work, and send money back home. When I let myself dream, I thought about owning my own store or nail salon, having a nice husband, and living in a clean house with two smart children.

When I first came to this country, I kept busy—nail colors changing, and flesh passing through my hands in miles and seconds, working at Pretty Nails, combing, and trimming private hair, yanking where the wax missed the single strands. I thought of my mother. My daughter, the one who became pregnant? She went to the United States to pluck pubic hair. I left to get away from the past, to make a new life. I used to wish my time would shrink to nothing but a sliver I could swallow. Now I surprise myself, after five years in the United States, I find spaces of time and distance exciting; life expands, it gets better.

When I first came to this country, I let my regrets ease out of me grain by grain. I hated being still. My family scraped together the money to give me an opportunity.

When I first came to this country, I never let myself remember.

*   *   *

Young marched off with his camera. I took off my backpack, tied my sweatshirt around my waist; a few minutes later, I followed him.

"What's wrong?" I asked. Young was frowning. His discontent amplified, his taciturn face reflected the flatness of the sandy brown earth walls.

"Nothing," he said. "I'm going to take some pictures." He went off and I saw flashes of his blue shirt, but he was far ahead, off the marked trail. I went back to the clearing and sat on a long wooden bench. I was angry, too.

Young's uncle is a priest; his entire family is Christian. They sing in the choir, make food for the church's Sunday lunch, collect money to send overseas to missions in Africa and the Philippines, and are Bible study leaders and altar boys. Please send us money for Sister Pamela's trip to the International Christian Fellowship conference in July. Your contribution is not about money, it's about doing God's work. If it isn't about money don't ask me for any, that's what I say. When I said that, Young got very angry.

It's stupid of me to be bullheaded. "There are things you say to get along," warned Soo. "Aiii! Your problem is you are too stubborn! So Korean! Why say anything? Just be both Christian and Buddhist. What's the problem? Just go through with it, maybe eventually you'll think it. Why make a stink and ruin everything? Just give five dollars. Here, I'll give it to you."

"No, no. I know. Okay, okay," I said.

Soo has many boyfriends so she gives me advice all of the time and says men are this way or that way and it's best not to say too much, or you should say more about this and not so much about that. I can never remember everything I'm supposed to do. The afternoon we first started to become friends was the day before I slept with Young for the first time. She gave me a bikini wax and I giggled because it tickled when she pressed hard on my flesh and kneaded it like a piece of dough.

"Are you going out soon?" asked Soo. "Looks like you have not done this."

"No."

"No, what?"

"No, I haven't done this. No, I'm not going out," I lied.

"Young is a very nice looking guy. Tall," she said with approval.

I looked down at the neatly trimmed triangle of hair and tried to envision Young's body without clothes and felt my face flush. I rushed to put on my clothes after the bikini wax and avoided the mirror across from me.

My reflection has changed. Now I look in the mirror and see my skin has smoothed out, the pink spots are gone, my cheeks are round. My eyes look relaxed, even happy. My ears are large, but my hair is long now and covers them nicely. Nancy told me that wide-set eyes are the best kind to have. I'll never be beautiful, but some people tell me that I'm pretty.

*　　　　　*　　　　　*

Sometimes I think of my old way, my old love: hot, sad, burnt black and dry. When Songsu put his hand on the nape of my neck, all breath left my body. Faith wrapped around me like a supple copper snake in the yellow warmth of the sun. Nine months later I held my baby for two hours in a blue blanket. Afterwards, I came to the U.S.

My mother's favorite and closest cousin married a man who owned a nail salon. They were rich. Every month the family received money from the U.S. Twice this cousin returned with money and presents of food, expensive cosmetics, shoes, all kinds of things. Relatives made plans to go to the U.S. but my parents kept postponing the move. My mother became ill. My grandmother died. My father gambled our savings. One relative returned after three years and said he hated it. I was lucky. On paper, at sixteen, I became the daughter of my mother's cousin and husband.

*　　　　　*　　　　　*

"You need a manicure," says Soo. "Your hands." My hands are rough from warm soapy water and cleaning the hands and feet of my customers. I lotion them constantly, smear petroleum jelly on them at night, but still they're callused and dry. After a day of manicures, pedicures, and waxes, I used to go downtown on Tuesdays and Thursdays to give massages and work at the baths. I quit over two months ago, yet my hands still look wrinkled and tired. I hide them carefully with long sleeves and never put anything but a clear polish on my nails. A faint blue vein snakes up the sides of my forearms. In the supermarket I stood behind a woman placing groceries on the counter. Her hands looked like mine but when she turned around I was shocked. The lines on her face matched her hands. They say you look at a woman's hands to tell her age. But I'm twenty-two and my hands look like someone who's forty.

Soo was happy when I told her that Young and I were going to the Grand Canyon. I won't tell my family about Young until we've begun to make wedding plans. Why say anything? Who tells everything anyway? I send my mother money once a month and I write about the United States. She would never believe the truth:

I pluck the pubic hairs of strange women.

I sleep with a man who hasn't yet married me.

I went to the Grand Canyon.

I imagine myself falling into the width of the United States and know I will never return to Korea.

I still think of my son.

What did Young expect? How can I believe in God just because he does? I couldn't see him taking pictures beyond the grove. I sat in a clearing near the bottom, drank my lukewarm water, and listened to the warbles of the birds and insects. The heat came down as I pulled crackers from my backpack and studied the pamphlet on the Grand Canyon. Bring plenty of water. Take frequent rests, especially during the heat of the day.

I reapplied sunscreen and hit a mosquito that came to rest on my knee. When I smashed it, a dot of blood appeared. I took a leaf from a tree and brushed it away, traces of the faint pink staining my skin. I squirted bottled water on it, scratched, and watched it defiantly swell. I stood up and began to search for Young, looking down the path and in the space between the branches for his blue shirt.

I envisioned a honeymoon with Young. I thought of lying on a deck chair in the sun on a TV ad luxury ocean liner. I made a note to move the cactus I had bought in Palm Springs to another window in my apartment. I recalled walking with my father as a small child and how when I was tired, he would put me on his shoulders and I would tightly hold his head, secure against his neck. Counting the arching trees, I stripped a stick of its bark, peeled it like an orange and let my thoughts march in steady circles.

*   *   *

When I grew up in Chinju, a small town far from Kwangju, the truth was never spared.

"She is ugly. Her face is like a big fish," said one aunt.

"Too bad your daughter looks like you," said my mother to my father.

"Work hard. Life is harder on a woman who is not beautiful," said my father.

"People are afraid of an honest face," said my grandmother.

"I think you're beautiful. Others may not see it, but it's because they are fooled by the obvious." I was told this by Songsu one dusk when it was about to rain thick and sweet. He was a university student and he impressed me with his talk about democracy and workers' rights. He was sent to organize demonstrations at the local clothing factory. My cousin found out about Songsu's identity, but by then Songsu had left town, chased out by the police. I knew he wouldn't come back. For Songsu, I did anything. It's hard to say who was to blame.

*   *   *

The sun was high. I thought of arguing with Young and pictured him falling off a rock, hiking further into the canyon, weaving his way into the large belly of earth without me. My armpits began to sweat, my face felt blue hot. Pushing through twigs, I dropped my bottle of water, tripped and scraped my knee and ran for a long time, stopping only to pick up a large stick I saw on the side of the path.

I started whacking the stick against a log, harder until it broke in two, calling out the names I had given my son over the years, names I had made up and written down on pieces of paper, on foggy windows, on the palm of my hands with my finger. I could hear my baby cry as the earth let me shake, guarding me like a fish with a tiny hatch of eggs in its mouth. I dove into the walls and became the dusty hooves of the mules and the moving river flanked by sweeping trees and tall grass. The eyes of my son and of Young passed through my heart, the animals howled and the pebbles were ground into powder as I walked back and forth. A sturdy cradle, the canyon saved me from falling.

I looked up and saw the woman from the path ten yards away, her smile was soft and open. She seemed to hover, part of the air and the earth, a floating presence without intrusion, just waiting there, softly. I wanted to run into her arms, but when I dried my face on my sleeves she had disappeared.

I circled back to where I dropped the water bottle and slumped down into a little ball. Young came through the clearing and found me curled on the stump. He put his arms around me. The park was empty. It was only Young and me and broken bones and living plants and light slicing sounds. I buried myself in his chest.

"Where were you? I couldn't find you," I said sobbing.

"I was taking pictures, I told you," he said softly. "I'm sorry Hana."

"I thought you left. I thought you were gone. I tried to follow you."

"I'm here, Hana."

"Are you sure?"

"Yes," said Young.

"Are you going?"

"Where would I go?" he said kissing me.

"I don't know," I mumbled. "I don't believe your God. I hate your God."

"It doesn't matter," he said soberly. "Please stop crying. I'm sorry. Don't be upset."

"You don't know," I said.

"It's not important."

The picture was taken at sunset. The rocks were a blood orange and the canyon seemed to undulate gently back and forth. I was buried down a deep tunnel or flying above; I was not there speaking. "I gave up my son," I cried. "I gave him up to be taken away. So I am here now. I'm telling you. I left a son behind before coming to the U.S., Young. I'm sorry. I'm sorry."

Young stood quietly and looked far away, as if he could see past the canyon, over the ocean and parched land, hundreds of miles away through the shuddering sky and falling clouds, and I heard him breathe. And for a moment, we were both a part of the earth.

THE KI DIFFERENCE

The bellhop throws them an indignant glance as they walk out the hotel lobby into the February cold of Seoul: an older Western man, a younger Korean woman. The pair hop a cab which drops them in front of a restaurant often frequented by tourists, a faded *New York Times* review from years before is proudly mounted by the entrance in a box of wood and glass.

Inside the door they take off their shoes. A hole in his socks reveals the nail of his big toe. The woman does not see this. If she did, it would certainly bother her.

"I knew he was the wrong guy the first time he showed up at the door in those overpriced athletic shoes," she had once said to a friend. "I ignored my gut instinct. Small details reveal everything."

The woman speaks to the hostess who ushers them to their seats. The man is a step behind the woman as they wind their way around lacquered tables and thick wooden posts. The floor is warm underneath their feet, and the smell of sesame comes from the back of the restaurant.

"Can you imagine this place in L.A.? It'd be better than Spago. Vegetarian food, this decor. We just pack this place up and move it to Beverly Hills. People would love it," says the man. At the table, they sit cross-legged on the floor.

"I like this place," says the woman. She points at the menu as the waitress scribbles down their order.

"It's so great. Hey there, this place is better than Spago! Hah, bet she liked that."

"She doesn't speak English, Dan." The waitress hurries towards the kitchen and comes back with a tray of a dozen small dishes which she expertly arranges on the table before walking away. The man immediately helps himself to a big mouthful of turnips and cabbage covered in a bright red pepper sauce.

"Thank you. Brilliant. Excuse me, miss. Miss. Miss. Excuse me, miss. Could I have some water, please? Miss?"

"Dan, I said she doesn't speak English."

"Just need some water. Miss, can I get some water over here? Service is definitely not like Spago's, I take that back. Eunice, can you pass some tea?"

"Dan, I told you. She doesn't speak English. She won't understand you just because you're saying it in a loud voice."

"I really love these tables. They're really cool. Just with this knee injury from Tae Kwan Do class a few weeks ago, it's a little tight."

"She's coming with some water. You look pink. Why don't you just uncross your legs?"

"Nah, I'm fine. We sit like this in class all the time. We had such a great workout two weeks ago. We had this visiting master, and he's doing the fight choreography on this film…"

"Do you need some more water? Are you okay, Dan?" she asks.

"I'm fine. Great. Fine. Really. How do you say thank you?"

"Koh-map-sub-nee-dah. Is the food too hot?"

"Koh-map-nee…Thanks so much. She's so cute. Food's fine."

"Here, have some of my water."

"Thanks. She looked a bit surly, didn't she?"

"They might not like all that winking. You're this Westerner, you know. She's Korean."

"Guess it's not L.A. Yeah, I understand. You look wonderful."

"How are your children?"

"Fine. Doing well."

"Good," she smiles. She notices for a second a pause in his breath. Their eyes briefly meet. His crow's feet deepen. Eunice coughs and remembers a much earlier conversation.

"You already had an entire life. I feel like everything would be a rerun with you," she had finally told him. "I'm closer in age to your son than I am to you."

"Don't be ridiculous," he had said, a slight tension in his voice. Irritation. Worry. He had tried to stare her down.

"I'm not," Eunice had said firmly. "It's the truth."

She knows Dan remembers the conversation.

"Everyone's doing great," says Dan. "You look wonderful."

"Thanks. Things are going well. I teach English, go to Korean language school classes. I share a place with two women, an African-American from Berkeley and a local. Got a year's visa. Things are going well," she repeats.

"Of course they are. This is a great country. Asia is great. Japan was fabulous. You would have really liked it. They are so polite."

"Where are you going tomorrow?"

"Singapore."

"The trip going well?"

"Yes, yes and no. They operate very differently, but I think we're getting someplace. Cutting deals. Bringing a little American style to Asia. I'm here for two weeks. Six countries."

"That's a lot. Do you need to get up and stretch your legs? You look pink."

"I think it's the kimchi."

"It's hot."

"No, I mean, I love hot food. All hot food. Just bring it on, baby. Actually, maybe it's just my stomach today." His face contorts.

"Are you sure you don't need a fork?" she asks.

"No, why are you asking?"

"The chopsticks are stainless steel and thin, so really, it is hard to get the hang of them cause they're so narrow. Even I had problems at first."

"No, I mean, geez. Listen babe, what kind of person do you think I am? Can't use chopsticks. Hello. You think I'm some kind of uncultured white guy?"

She pauses. He looks awkward with his bent knees, his loud voice shouting in English. Was he like this all along? She can't remember.

"I'm not saying that. I'm just saying that they're hard to use. They have forks I'm sure, since this is a tourist place."

"No, I'm fine."

"Sure?"

"Maybe I'll get a fork."

"Sure, pork-uh-choo-say-yo."

"Oh my god, you speak so well. You look so cute speaking Korean."

"I speak shitty Korean. What do you mean I look cute speaking Korean? I am Korean. Korean-American." The waitress places a fork by Dan's bowl.

"I know. Thank you, miss. How do you say thank you? Tha-nk-you!" He smiles and claps his hands together, bows his head and closes his eyes.

"Ko-map-sub-nee-dah. Don't bow like that."

"What do you mean?"

"They don't do that here. She'll think you're a weirdo. They only do that hands-together-bow thing in bad kung fu movies."

"I was being polite."

"Well, it's silly. I know you're being nice. But they don't get it. And Dan…"

"Yeah?"

"Don't wink at her. She doesn't get it. She probably thinks you're a pervert."

"I am."

"Yeah, I know, but just leave her alone."

"You know, the Japanese are just wonderful. Koreans too. You're all incredible."

She slowly sips her tea before saying, "You know, I'm okay here."

"You seem it." He reaches across the table and pats her hand.

"I feel content here. Just…I don't miss L.A. It sounds strange, I know."

She remembers their conversations about traveling. Dan had promised to take her to Europe. Then, they were going to see the Great Wall. Maybe climb a pyramid. They went to Palm Springs instead. She remembers the sweat underneath her knees and in the bend of her elbow, her shirt sticking to her back like clear plastic wrap.

The desert was burning, and Eunice had said she wanted to try frying an egg on the pavement, but Dan didn't want to stop. He said he would fry himself if he had to get out of the air-conditioned car. They had checked into a hotel, and Eunice jumped on the big bed with the ugly flower bedspread, bouncing up and down until Dan got on and hit his head on the ceiling. Later that evening, they ate hamburgers and walked underneath the steam of the outdoor air conditioning, and Dan recited the whole ending scene from *Casablanca* by heart through the mist, and Eunice had laughed. She insisted that Dan take her picture by Sonny Bono's Walk of Fame star. "I got you babe," Dan had sung. And then they drank margaritas and stumbled back to the hotel and collapsed on the bed. Eunice had flinched when they checked out and the hotel clerk called her Mrs. Sommers.

"That's beautiful. I belong here too! I mean, we both like it here. I feel content, too. I mean, really at peace…all of that zen stuff, just really comes through here in Asia in a major way. What's this?"

"Tofu."

"Oh, I love tofu."

"They make it in shapes like meat because this is a vegetarian place."

"Love it. Ha! What's the calorie count? Just joking. This tea is even great. Maybe we should just do the tearoom setup in Silver Lake or maybe Westside. Trendy but ever so, so . . . zen," says Dan and laughs. "I have this personal tea mixture this old Chinese guy brews for me in Santa Monica, and it's great, but I love this decor. Very cool. Nice restaurant you have. Superb tea! Just love it."

"Dan, I told you, they don't understand English. Have a cookie."

"That's okay. Watching my sugar intake. Protein really does the trick. Lost five pounds just increasing the protein. Kills the sugar craving. What's wrong?"

"I'm fine."

"You look like you've got something on your mind."

"No, nothing." She notices gray hair around his temples. His eyes are lighter. She remembers the last time she saw him—he had made it a point to outrun her on the beach.

Her friend had told her, "Old dudes do things like that to prove they still have it. I guarantee that any normal guy your age wouldn't give a shit if you outran him on the beach. Hell, I'd let a woman outrun me on the beach—better view."

"You just fit with this room. I mean it is so right for you," says Dan.

"What are you talking about?"

"There, next to the vase. You look great."

"I have to go to the restroom." She walks to the back of the restaurant and returns just as a waitress stops in front of their table to pour him tea.

"Cookie's not bad. You know Eunice, I am Western, but I've always thought of myself as having an Eastern sensibility. That's why I started studying the martial arts. Plus, I really dig Japanese design. Philosophically I feel Asian. I'm Jewish, but I really feel comfortable here. Asians are my tribe."

"You've only been here for two days."

"I've been in Asia almost a week. A week can be a long time."

"A week can be a long time—sometimes. Try it for three months. You might feel differently. It's not that easy, really."

Eunice signals to the waitress for their check.

"I don't know, I could absorb some of this inner wisdom. Lots of business. Just the people. Beautiful. I'm getting tired. Can we get the check? Check. Check. Check."

"Dan, they don't speak...oh, forget it."

They exit the restaurant heading out into the wind and slushy streets. They enter the hotel, and the bellhop focuses his irritation on his clipboard. The man marches ahead, pressing the elevator button, all smiles as he holds the elevator door for the woman and politely bowing as another man exits. On a panel inside the elevator are scenes from Versailles. A rendering of Marie Antoinette is in the center. A lady-in-waiting wears a white powdery wig with a pink bird in the middle, her hairdo looking as if it might topple her body over.

"Bad hair day," Eunice says pointing to the portrait.

"I'll say." Dan casually touches a thin spot on the back of his head.

She follows him into the room and plops herself in the chair by the window and gazes out at the skyline of dim gold lights as he hangs up his jacket and goes to the bathroom. A tremendous flush sounds, then the whoosh of the faucet. The door opens and he emerges, a look of slight relief on his face. She clicks through the stations one by one, remote control in hand, stopping briefly to watch the AFKN channel: GIs warned to dress warmly to protect themselves against colds and flu. The room smells of cleaning detergent; the musty carpet emits a slightly damp odor. The wallpaper's gold threads run in diamond patterns up and down the wall. She takes off her coat.

"I've been studying a little with this ki kong practitioner. Trying to learn about moving the ki, that's chi in Korean, ki, and he says some pretty interesting things," she says.

"We have so much in common. I've totally been doing the same thing." He fumbles through his suitcase and pulls out a pair of sunglasses.

"Ki kong?"

"No, these. From Sharper Image. Try them. It's exactly like meditation."

"What are they?"

"They are very expensive glasses. I paid a small fortune for them. You watch this pattern, and it affects your synapses. It's a meditation device. You put them on and it's like you're sent to another plane. It's better than meditation because your brain is receiving stimulus. Five-hundred bucks worth."

"You paid five-hundred dollars to buy this thing to meditate? Hah."

"Try it. Don't knock it."

"I thought meditation was staying still. I ate a lot. I feel really full," sighs Eunice. Brand-Name-Dan she had once called him, though never to his face: BMW, Adidas, Rolex, American Express Platinum card, Gucci.

"I'm a generic brand kind of person. I think brand names are silly," she had said to him after a lecture he gave her about the impression cars make. "I'm not a car person."

Dan had laughed. "Don't limit yourself, Eunice. You deserve more out of life."

He says it again now, "Don't limit yourself, Eunice. Don't have such a narrow definition of meditation. Here, try it. Lie down. Put these glasses on."

Eunice sits on the bed. "Okay. Hey, don't rub my shoulders." She moves away from him and looks through the glasses. "These are odd."

Dan stands up and mutes the TV. "Here, try it with my CD player. Then you get the full effect." He puts earphones in her ears as she lies down.

"These are unrelaxing. God, Dan. They make me feel tense. Don't you feel dizzy? They're stressful. That pattern swirling around is like a bad music video or something." She takes off the glasses, removes the earphones, and hands it all back to him. "They're well—they're just not for me."

"Let me take them. I happen to really like them," he says defensively. Dan puts on the glasses, turns his back towards her, and lies on the bed.

On a small table sit two beautiful boxes wrapped in thin rice paper, a black cord tied round them; calligraphy swirling in black and red decorates the top. Eunice walks over and sits in the chair and unwraps a box. "What are these boxes?"

"The Japanese gave me them yesterday." His eyes absorb the patterns in the glasses. He fiddles with the earphones.

"Do you mind if I unwrap them?"

"Just one." He doesn't look at her and talks to the ceiling.

"Yum. Mochi." She takes a deep breath and bites into one, glancing at Dan on the bed in his brown pants and white shirt. New shoes of tight brown leather. His tie is a small furious knot against his neck. She takes a second mochi. "Dan, can I eat one?"

"Go ahead."

Before finishing her second, she contemplates a third. She takes a nibble out of one and puts it back in the box. She knows he will be slightly disgusted if he sees this. "Pretty boxes."

"The Japanese were great."

"You do that a lot?"

"Every day."

"You're not serious."

"It's meditation. I'm going to turn up the volume."

"Great view." She switches on the volume of the TV, then decides to mute it and looks out the window, breathing on the cold glass, fogging up the corner. She writes "Eunice was here" and turns up the TV volume. A game show. A talk show. An American film. The news. He begins to snore.

"Dan?" She turns off the TV, slips the opened box of mochi under her arm, grabs her coat. "Dan?" He gives a slight snort in his sleep. Glasses on, legs splayed. She spots a slight tug on the lower buttonhole of his shirt where his stomach is stretching the fabric.

She remembers how he had tanned himself on an orange raft in Palm Springs, floating on water under the white desert sun. The floor of the pool was painted like an ocean. She splashed and made waves from the deep end and the raft gently rocked. She swam in circles and pretended to be a shark, and when she surfaced he laughed and promised to build her a marble swimming pool.

She closes her eyes and imagines she sees the circle pattern of Dan's glasses, as if she looked at the sun too long; little black dots floating by spinning pinwheels and Dan a blob of muted colors in her peripheral vision. He snores soundly—a machine, a trumpet, a low fart. She walks silently to the doorway, switches off the lights, and closes the door.

HONG KONG REBOUND

I hold my father's hand as we approach a red building near the escalator, a bar in Central. He explains to me, this is where the rich foreigners drink and watch football. My father cannot afford to drink here, nor would he be welcome if he stepped foot inside. Years later I will come to this very bar with colleagues from work and will hesitate before the door, remembering the time I stood outside with my father.

Tall foreign men lumber in and out with loosened ties and long-sleeved shirts of white and light blue. Their pointed noses and large soft bodies are unlike my father's; his nose is flat and firm, and his body is lean and tan from carrying ladders and boards, hauling pails and scrubbing with rags. He's a head shorter than the men inside, but his fist is wide, and his arms and calves bulge from work. An odd-job jack-of-all-trades, he washes dishes in offices, fixes broken furniture and paints—anything to make money. The foreign men blurt out words in a language I can't understand and will struggle for years to study in school: I couldn't believe it. Sounds like a good deal. It's the direction. Bloody hell. Their voices undulate as the door swings back and forth, opening and shutting. Blasts of cool air shoot out and hit my calves, the smell of stale beer tickles my nose and I sneeze to push out the stench of alcohol.

He has come here before without me to watch a game, but a week ago my mother left Hong Kong for her small village off the coast of Shanghai to tend to my sick grandmother. Holding me in his arms he says, look at the TV Mee-ling, watch the men in red uniforms. Look, look. Look at the ball. I say, ball? My father points to the ball on TV and we watch together, but it's hard for me to see, so I squirm and he puts me down on the ground.

This is before my brothers are born, and my father is tall with hope, not stooped like the handle of an umbrella, eyes folded over, double lidded from long hours of work. My slender mother, who turns heads as she walks down the street, smiles when she sees my father and does not avert her eyes with disappointment when he tries to speak with her. When he brings me presents—barrettes, shiny white vinyl sandals, a small stuffed lion, my mother exclaims in mock protestation, Mee-ling will be spoiled, what good is a spoiled girl? But she's happy. Unlike her sister's husband who complains about his houseful of daughters, my father brags about me and until next year when my brother is born, I am everything to him.

I hold my arms up to him to be carried. He picks me up but only to sit me on a wooden chair under the stairs of the escalator. He scuttles over to peer through the window again. Yowling pierces the air. Behind a gray metal fence are cats arching their backs—one black, one gray, staring at each other, locked in frozen anger. People gather and wait for the fight to begin. My father cups his hands against the glass for a better view of the game and stands on his toes, but I climb down off my chair and toddle over to the cats. When my father remembers to check on me, he briefly panics until he spots me by the fence hidden amongst thighs and legs. He pulls me away from the crowd and hugs me with relief. As the yowling hits a frenzied pitch and the gray cat strikes the black, he hoists me on to his shoulders and says, let's watch the game together and after, we can eat noodles. I clutch his head, pulling at his spiky black hair as he hurries back to the window.

Deep voices rise from the belly of the bar, baritone shouts break in a chorus of cheers scattering over the din of jackhammers and taxicabs, the clack of high-heel shoes and blare of air conditioners. Goal! My father excitedly rattles away to the circle of men who stand outside with him arguing, dragging on cigarettes and shuffling their feet. The men in red uniforms are pouncing on top of each other. Say hello uncle, says my father. Hello uncle, I say, to no uncle in particular. The uncles smile.

My father wears green shorts, a red striped shirt and thick navy blue rubber-soled sandals. On his brow are drops of salty sweat. His big toenail is purple, recently smashed by a hammer. When he comes home, I run to see it for he has told me that soon, the purple toe will turn into a bunch of grapes. Every day I look to see if the grapes have appeared, but no, it is the same toe, turning mushroom black.

One smiling uncle says, whoever heard of bringing a girl to watch a game? He pulls a stick of chewing gum from his shirt pocket and I let go of my father's head to reach for the gum and his arms tighten around my legs. The sugar coats my tongue, and I clap my hands and the man, Chewing Gum Uncle, chuckles with pleasure.

I'm looking at the men inside, holding glasses and bottles with open mouths and knitted brows. Their eyes follow the small figures on-screen racing across a green carpet in pursuit of the ball. They wince as a player falls to the ground. To most of the foreign men, the uncles and myself are invisible, mere background, a backdrop to important lives, like the smell of car exhaust and old orange peels, the chill of an air-conditioned shop or the postcard stretch of towers of mirror and steel that puncture the sky. A pale fat man grins and waves to me. I wave back. Some scowl when they see us. One deliberately moves in front of the window, his white shirt and thick neck blocking our TV view. A few of the uncles leave just as two men with faces flushed pink from alcohol exit the bar and head towards the stairs to take the escalator up the hill.

My father swears under his breath and I am jostled as he and Chewing Gum Uncle move to another window, craning their necks to see the TV. The goalkeeper is no good, says my father. Chewing Gum Uncle grimaces and says, the problem is the defense. Oh! Good! Penalty kick. Chewing Gum Uncle nods and my father says, c'mon, kick the ball. Suddenly a young red-haired man pushes his nose up against the windowpane and snorts at my father. I let out a cry and feel my father's body stiffen as he steps back, shushes and comforts me. In the glass I see my father's reflection, his steady eyes, his mouth drawn in a stern straight line. The men inside laugh at us—one guffaws and slaps the red-haired man on the back. Chewing Gum Uncle says good-bye and pats my leg before walking away. A wavy-haired man with no chin tries to shoo us away like flies. My father's hold on my calves tightens and he watches the screen and ignores them. The red-haired man laughs again. He scares me. I want to get down from my father's shoulders but he says sharply, be still. The chinless man shakes and growls like a dog at a young Asian woman who cowers before him.

A few minutes later, the woman tapes a piece of black paper to the window with masking tape. The TV light cuts through a small tear. My father moves to another spot, but the woman seems to follow us steadily from window to window, without ever meeting our eyes, covering each section of glass. The men inside barely glance at us; expressionless, they slowly disappear behind a black curtain of paper.

My father's shoulders drop and round when we can no longer see the screen. He slumps and puts me down on the ground. His face looks tired; this is the first time I see the expression he will come to almost always wear. He pulls my braided hair and looks at the blacked-out windows, and when I see his long eyes I ask about the TV, but he doesn't respond. I reach for his hand, then soberly he says that it is time for us to go home. From behind the black paper, inside the bar there are whoops, claps and cries of joy. My father's eyes lift, a rebound, a brief light returns and he slowly gathers me in his arms. He says, time for noodles. I nod my head and look down at his toenail and wonder when the grapes will appear.

NANTUCKET'S LAUNDRY, 1985

I was sitting on the ferry from Woods Hole to Nantucket, trying to devise a way for Ted to notice me. All I saw were his mirrored sunglasses, which could not conceal his beautiful face, a crown of golden hair, and a cigarette emerging from the corner of his smooth-lipped mouth.

I was pretending to read a book that years later would fall out of my window onto a back-alley rooftop. Irretrievable and slowly disintegrating, I forgot about it until my brother Michael told me that Ted had killed himself by jumping from his mother's New York 57th street penthouse. The news triggered the taste of ocean salt and his sun drenched supple body and caused my head to throb with recollection. It had been more than a decade since that Nantucket summer, and by then, I no longer knew Ted, nor had I thought of him for many years, but his death gave me pause; it reminded me that there was a time when I did not hesitate in love, did not understand inhibition, and dared to question the contradictions of innocence and bravery.

That long ago day on the ferry, Ted was watching me. I thought this peculiar given my ongoing battle with a recent lopsided perm. At seventeen, my pre-orthodontic grin was crooked but enthusiastic, and while my looks were the type that my mother assured me I would "grow into," Ted exuded the fearless wonder of youth and privilege.

His stance told me that to flirt with someone with his perceived mystique and definite physique was an audacious move on my part, but the coolness of the Atlantic swaddled me with a delicious chill and imbued me with bravery. I felt carefree and confident in my decision to wear a tight tank top that emphasized the rise of my breasts and had the added bonus of squeezing my round stomach under my jean jacket, rather than the one turtleneck packed for cool evenings on the beach.

I stepped out onto the deck and leaned against the railing, scanning the page for a run of dialogue to anchor my wandering eye. As the sweet sun heated my face, I glanced down at the white edge of foam framing the wave and the possibilities of the summer rolled before me. It was barely the first of May, a month before Nantucket's season officially began, but I was determined to get an early start.

Nantucket had been my plan to escape the confines of home before going to state university that fall. To my surprise, my parents agreed. I had skipped two grades and they felt the summer would be a time for me to mature and make money, a practical reward for a year spent obediently following the plans they had laid for me as a community college student and intern at the local newspaper's art department. When my friends visited from college I had felt younger for not having left home. Dorms. Drinking. Sex. Nantucket would be my chance to experience adulthood and independence.

My brother Michael was the pre-med student at Cornell upon whom my parents projected their immigrant dreams of success; by contrast, I was the daughter who aspired to be an artist, an idea that made my Confucian father shake his head when he contemplated the impracticality of such a pursuit. It was my burden to live in my brother's shadow and to accept without complaint the privileges bestowed upon a first-born male; my brother's burden was to prove to my parents that he was deserving of every sacrifice they had made over the years. Michael was a student at Phillips Academy Andover located in the Massachusetts town where I, a "townie," attended the local high school. By the time I was old enough to go, my parents felt private school tuition wasn't worth the expense, especially after Michael didn't get into Harvard. And so it was that I came to look upon such gates of entitlement with a strange mixture of familiarity, curiosity, and resentment.

When Ted flashed a warm grin and sat across from me to look out on the horizon, he appeared before me like my answer from the gods, exuding summer and release, adventure and desire. I felt a nervous rush of adrenaline surge in his presence and could feel his eyes scan my body as I angled it towards him. I found myself smiling as he pulled off his sunglasses, my posture shifting as I deliberately exposed my shoulder blade and pulled my tank top tighter against my breasts. As the small flock leaving the ferry began to disperse, I stalled, slowed my walk to a ponderous pace, pulled out a worn address book from my backpack, and pretended to search for a name.

I wanted him with a burst of denial and simultaneous dread, and before I knew it, a few questions soon led pretty Ted to say: "I know this is kind of strange, but if you don't have a place to stay, you could stay at mine. I got the rental early; my roommates won't be here 'til Memorial Day."

"Sure," I said, hoping he thought it was the biting wind turning my face pink.

I tried to convince myself it didn't mean anything as a few inquiries revealed that he vaguely knew Michael from a class at Andover. They hadn't been friends, but I guessed that Ted's hospitality could be chalked up to preppy behavior—doing favors and opening doors; behavior I had enviously observed when around my brother and his friends.

Ted and I spent the night in the empty beach house, drinking beer and eating pizza, stepping outside to gaze at the crisp stars dropped in the hollow of the night, our eyes opening in applause. I found myself chatting at rapid speed when he leaned over to kiss me.

"Have you ever kissed an Asian before?" I blurted, waiting for the response that would reveal me as an aberration in what I perceived to be Ted's life—one gloriously free of difference and the questions of belonging.

"No. Does it matter? I'm kissing *you*, Lydia. Have you ever kissed someone white?" he asked thoughtfully.

"Yeah," I said. *Once in the first grade.*

"I don't mind," said Ted.

"What's that supposed to mean?"

"I guess, it just doesn't really matter. Are you liking it?"

"Yes."

As our clothes came off, we reached and arched and turned. I felt his mouth on my neck, ran my hands over his chest and thighs, and felt him pull my body into his skin and flesh. Hips touching, I couldn't tell whose it was, mine or his, but it didn't matter.

During the nights and days that followed, we partied and played with others who were making their way to the island for summer. My roommate was Amanda, a jewelry maker with sandy brown ringlets and a high-pitched giggle who worked at a deli across from the Royal Saloon where I worked as a waitress. Friends flitted from parties to work, camaraderie the dollar, the beach, and the romance of the long summer stretched out before us.

Ted had taken the semester off from Princeton where he was studying architecture to travel to Europe and had plans to apprentice with a local furniture maker. We discussed future plans and I too, felt the possibilities lap at the shore. We ate steamers, drank Cape Codders, and exchanged witticisms, making up voices and rules and laughing only long enough to come up for air before another exuberant embrace. Running out onto the sand dunes, we watched the small waves dance and break, chased each other into the water, and licked the salt from each other's skin. Hiding in our bodies, racing to take off our clothes, arms and legs pliant and warm like pretzels, we watched golden flecks bounce off our bodies browned from the sun.

"I like your eyes. The blue is pretty," I said.

"I like yours."

"All Asians have my eyes," I said, shying from his compliment.

"Can't Asians have different eyes?"

"I guess," I said, scarlet faced. I didn't believe what I said and was embarrassed that I said it.

"I like your eyes. They say things," said Ted softly.

The island was a postcard of quaint clapboard homes and cobblestone streets, clean Atlantic air filling me with nostalgia before I experienced the event. Days off meant biking and swimming with evening keggers on the beach and a dance at a club. Ted and I strolled along the sand and watched the sunset and I reveled in acting out my summer movie. The soundtrack swelled. Credits rolled. Patrons smashed the popcorn on the sticky cement floor and walked out into the sun that stabbed their eyes.

"This family friend came on Island and mentioned Dad got married to another woman," said Ted disgustedly.

"He didn't tell you he got married?"

"No. And the point is that he's a money hungry asshole. My father told me he married my mom because he was broke, and that would be the only reason he would ever marry, ever. Mom is on drugs and a bitch; who'd want to marry her? He only screws rich women and that includes my mother, who frankly deserves the worst."

When the weather turned, we sat on the dunes and huddled like birds in a scooped-out basin. I leapt up from the sand and spun in circles and sprawled out like a starfish as tiny silken grains slid off my ankles and filled my hair.

"What are you doing?" said Ted laughing.

"Getting dizzy," I said.

"Weirdo."

"Better than being boring. I'd hate to be old and boring."

"I can't imagine you boring or old. Shit, I feel old. Not always, but I'm not a young one like you," said Ted somberly.

"How do you think you're gonna die? Young or old?"

"Weird question… maybe in the middle of an orgasm. Young."

"You're pathetic."

"Maybe old. Sex doesn't stop. Dad's wife is my age."

"You're sick. I think I'll die in some weird way," I said, thinking of the murders I had read about in the horror magazines stacked in my bedroom closet at home.

"My uncle hung himself."

"Geez."

"My grandma said he was too sensitive. She said when he was a kid he even cried at the zoo 'cause the animals were locked up in cages. She said it was the monkeys. Actually, it's not funny," he said frowning at my laughter. The wind took a rest. Ted sorrowfully looked out at the water.

"I'm sorry."

"Forget it. I used to think about suicide. Everyone does, you know. But I haven't recently. You get used to it all."

"I know what you mean," I said, absorbed in my own worries. Recent family turmoil had centered around Michael's girlfriend Stacey, a pre-law student and the daughter of wealthy Jamaican real estate developers. Stacey was black. Dad had threatened to disown him; Michael had stopped calling, and Mom was crying on the phone to me. I didn't tell Michael about Ted. I knew what my brother would say.

"You couldn't possibly. People do things that you could never understand."

"What do you mean?" I asked defensively.

"You just can't. Maybe it's because your family is not as fucked up as mine. But deep down people are always the same. Assholes. What the hell do you know?"

Ted's anger seemed to devour his very flesh, and I acquiesced in silence. All I knew was that he had a way of slowly peeling my skin until I was a quivering jellyfish floating with the tides, a clear surface that split when I dove. I was swimming in his deep, my toes unable to touch the sand, my lungs ready to burst, determination scratching and stinging my legs as I kicked. I picked up a handful of sand and threw it at him, and we wrestled in the sand before he pinned me on my back.

"I'm sorry," he said.

"Forget it."

"I'm just some old bitter fart. You're a young one, I should be more kind." He patted me and looked out at the water.

"Hey, you're only three years older than I am," I said.

He kissed me and paused and squeezed my hand. "True. Lydia—I have this girlfriend but we're kind of taking a break from each other."

"Oh," I said my stomach dropping.

"Martha was a girlfriend of mine at Andover. We've been on and off for a few years."

"Oh?"

"I mean, nothing's definite in terms of her coming to Nantucket."

"Come catch me!" I didn't want to hear him, so I turned away, stripped off my clothes and hurled myself into water so cold it cut my flesh. Ted ran up to the water's edge with my sweater and held my shivering body. "I'm freezing to death," I gasped.

"No, shit," he said laughing.

"You know what your problem is? You're uptight," I said relieved that the subject had changed.

"One of us has to be."

The day his friends came on Island, I spent the night in my apartment alone. Amanda was at her new boyfriend Kevin's. Thereafter I saw Ted sporadically after the bars closed. He would ride up on his motorcycle, shout up to the window, and I would open the back door. Reeking of alcohol and cigarettes, he would stumble up the steps and we would hungrily cling to each other, as if to squeeze the hope and life from our bodies, crashing into a deep sleep and reluctantly awakening early the next morning, the taste and feel of sex on our bodies, in our mouths, and on our necks. He would leave with a friendly unsentimental good-bye and a bare mention of seeing each other in the future. After the door closed, I would go back to bed for a few minutes, feeling the warm spot on the sheets, smelling him on the pillows and blankets, closing my eyes and touching my own skin, still tingling from the night before.

Ted kept a strict distance from me in public. Yet, it was difficult for me to piece together how this came about; who started this mutual dislike— was he like this all along?

"Jesus, Lydia, I mean the guy was always a jerk," said Michael over the phone with exasperation.

"No, he wasn't."

"He's a typical white prep. Not worth it."

"No—"

"They're assholes and racists. And I'm moving in with Stacey. Fuck 'em," said Michael.

Ted's absence from my daily life marked a turn in the season. Without him I became aware of my difference and so did others, or so it seemed. Summer revelry began to sour. Amanda and I were arguing about her boyfriend Kevin, who had moved into our apartment. I was fired from the Royal Saloon, and though I hated the job, I was mad when Amanda took my place.

I hadn't talked to Ted in weeks when he called. "They're my favorite pair," he said.

"I thought you were trying to defy your stereotype."

"I like them. Plus, they're monogrammed at the bottom. They gotta be around your apartment someplace. Martha gave them to me."

"Maybe you lost them when you went skinny-dipping out at Madaket." I picked up his shorts and studied the hand-embroidered name *Martha* next to a tiny mallard duck on the waistband.

"I'd appreciate it if you would tell me if they show up," said Ted politely.

"No prob, but they're not here."

By late July I began work as a housecleaner for the realty companies. The rental homes were decorated with an uncanny uniformity. Tasteful, predictable, and practical homes held wicker furniture with firm chintz cushions, dog-eared paperbacks of *Moby Dick* perched on oak bookshelves, shiny copper kettles atop white stoves, and braided rag rugs strewn across smooth wooden floors. The walls sounded off echoes of platitudes about *how things are done*, debates about sailing and the proper books to read, and careful analysis based on family experience about Milton, Deerfield, or Andover. I tried to imagine something ugly or sordid occurring within the walls of those homes, but I never could, as if the armor protecting the righteous and deserved were well-worn corduroys, Brooks Brothers sweaters, and blemish-free complexions.

As I dusted the picture frames and polished the furniture, I could hear Ted reminisce in a faltering voice about the few summers his family spent on Nantucket before his dad had a breakdown and left. Ted had showed me the photograph of his handsome silver-haired father and his new wife—a year older than Ted, she was a fashion model and the daughter of a shipping magnate.

"She married my father because her own dad hates him," explained Ted.

Big Balding Bill, a middle-aged bouncer who spent his days working in the bike shop, was an exception to the palette of heather blonds and baby blues. He was one of the few black year-long residents, and could be spotted cast fishing along the beaches in the early foggy morning. He was known by the community as a decent fellow who kept to himself, a quality that probably made him all the more acceptable to the islanders. One night when I went up to the bar for a beer, I passed a table of men I had seen come into the Royal Saloon—daytrippers I guessed, though later I learned a few were seasonal workers like myself.

"Ah-sooo," said one with a snicker. A low murmur was followed by "chink," uttered loud enough to cause me to march back to the table.

"What the hell was that?" I growled. Barely audible denials met my anger. One man grinned, another sneered, yet another stood, mouth agape in the shape of a perfect oval. "Fuck you!" I said.

A few chuckled. "I didn't say anything."

"Someone was saying something, assholes. And I'm not a chink, you fuckers. I'm Korean."

I promptly reported the incident to Bill who lumbered over to express his displeasure in a few quiet syllables; the men left the bar en masse.

I would see the men skulk and slither past the Royal Saloon and felt satisfaction knowing that they felt foolish in my presence, yet in truth it was their victory. My charge led them to back down, but their actions made me hesitant about meeting people the rest of the summer, a fear I disguised by arrogance and wisecracks. I spun thin strings of protection into a sturdy cocoon, nurtured my defiance, and learned how to collapse into an invisible tiny ball that even friends couldn't open.

The only other Asian on Island was a young Filipina who worked behind the soda fountain in the town's main drugstore. From her accent, clothes, and hairstyle I knew she was a recent immigrant, "unassimilated" —the kind who often showed up in my family's living room and with whom I was obliged to socialize with, but never introduced to my friends. We barely acknowledged each other, yet it was the only place I sat in public without feeling uncomfortable. I passed many hours reading at that drugstore, sipping chocolate ice cream sodas, staring out the window, and scribbling away in my journal on the pink Formica table. I came to know her name because someone called me Frances and asked when I quit my job at the soda fountain.

I wish I could say that I answered smartly back, "No, you have the wrong Asian," but I didn't. I said: "My name's Lydia."

I got a second job at Nantucket's public laundromat to supplement my income cleaning houses. I made a dollar above minimum wage and worked folding sheets and clothes with Friendly Felicia—a high school senior, Big Balding Bill's niece and the only black girl I saw all summer on Nantucket, and Simple Edie—a strawberry blonde college student whose family had summered on Island since she was a baby.

Helen, my cigarette-smoking boss, was a divorcée with a tough accent that demarked her Gloucester, Massachusetts origins. Her dad was a second generation Portuguese fisherman, her mom, she said proudly, was a *good old-fashioned Boston Irish Catholic girl, god-bless-her.* For the past fifteen years, the profitable summer months had subsidized the rest of Helen's year.

The surroundings were pleasant. Bright sunlight came in through the open doors and windows and the linoleum floors were swept and mopped every day. Flowers of peach and blue grew along the fence, and the dusty gravel road by the entrance was filled with a constant stream of bicycles and cars driving in and out.

"At the end of the season, I throw a party for my girls. You might not make as many tips as you do down on Main Street, but it's steady work, and I'm flexible. Plus, you can do your laundry for free," she said, puffing away at the entrance under the 'No Smoking' sign.

"You're good at this," said Helen approvingly. There was a system to doing the laundry. We separated colors and whites before throwing the laundry into the wash; then before transferring the load to the dryer, we shook out the wrinkled clothes. After forty-three minutes the buzzer would sound and the folding would begin. If jeans took longer, we might run the dryer longer, or lay them on top of the machine to grab some warmth. Socks were folded into thirds like compact squares, underwear into tiny neat quarters; bras straps were smartly tucked into the cups. We were wash, dry, and fold only. No ironing. "And you don't need to," said Helen firmly. "If you do the washing and drying properly, that is, fold as soon as you take it out."

I folded sheets with Friendly Felicia whose thick glasses and endless high school chatter I found amusing and all too reminiscent of a recent past. She had olive skin and thick wavy black hair and a large collection of hair ribbons. Simple Edie was all pink and shiny blonde. Her welcoming smile was genuine, but I found her dull and slow-witted. After her fourth recap of her French shopping trip my vituperative tongue gave way.

"You make France sound like a mall."

I watched Simple Edie's face fall and quickly said, "I'm joking, Edie. I'm sorry, I'm just tired today." I bought her a muffin at lunchtime and folded sheets with her the rest of the day.

We folded fitted sheets by matching up the elasticized corners, carefully aligning the elasticized white strips and white seams corner to corner. The sheet would then be folded until it was a neat rectangle; to this day, I fold my sheets the way Helen taught me.

Every day I swept the floors, did laundry, took my lunch break out in the garden, and watched the people come into the laundromat. The job was monotonous, but even worse, when I told friends or acquaintances I was working at the laundromat they appeared baffled. My new job was not the prestige position I once held as a Royal Saloon waitress. Weeks had passed since I saw Ted, but like everyone else who worked on the island, he showed up at the laundromat.

"Lydia, when did you start working here?" Ted asked in disbelief. He gave a laugh. Not a snicker, but more than a snort, a voice pushing the edge of disdain.

"A while ago. Not long." I went to the small back room and pretended to look for the broom. "I'm going for lunch, Helen," I announced. *Lydia The Laundry Lady.* Helen waved me off and I put on my sunglasses, hopped on my bike, and pedaled away. Ted had made me flush a scarlet shame: My arrogance and pride. My humility and desire. My reward and embarrassment.

By the time I had returned, Nick The Gardener was at work mowing the lawn. Under Nick's care, Helen's verdant garden was gloriously healthy. He planted rows of orange patience and bachelor's buttons, trimmed the bushes, watered the grass, and repainted the white picket fence. Nick had a deep baritone voice, a reddish beard, and pink, not bronze skin. He wore a dirty Oakland A's baseball cap and his fingers were thick and short. Familiar and easy, everything he was and believed showed on his face.

"Helen, you are going to have the most amazing compost pile. The best on the island," said Nick.

"Your pile. I'm not one for worms. You take care of it," Helen said, shaking her head and walking inside.

"Helen, Fair Queen of the Compost. Alas, I am merely Nick, her lowly and grunged out serf."

"I'm her serf, too," I said giggling.

"You can be the Compost Princess."

"I'm not into monarchy."

"Okay, serf. Or 'serf-ette,'" joked Nick.

"What the hell is a serf-ette?"

"A modern female serf. Not to be confused of course, with a 'surfer babe' or a suffragette, although all good serfs do vote," he quipped.

Nick was going back to Santa Barbara in the fall to finish his degree in environmental science. I began to anticipate the days we sat outside together for lunch. He brought his laundry by on the days he worked on the lawn, but instead of asking me to take care of it like others I knew had begun to do, he politely dropped it in a pile. I knew he liked me, but I closed my body to him and guarded my movements, avoiding conversation that had any nuance of sexual innuendo.

A week later I found myself at the soda fountain talking to a young woman with a luminous face and skinny legs and arms. With her evenly worn Levi's cutoffs, a forest green L.L. Bean backpack, and a two-tone Rolex strapped on her wrist, she was a poster child for the New England good life, right down to her name—Martha. I could tell at best we would be acquaintances, classroom equals who respected each other's intellect, but under no circumstances would we be friends. When she stood near me I could smell the thick and powdery scent of Ralph Lauren Polo. I had to suppress a sneeze.

"I'd do anything. I haven't ever worked before, or I mean for a restaurant before, so I probably couldn't be a waitress," she said, swinging her long sunlit hair. Her pert freckled nose and blue eyes were friendly.

"I used to work at the Royal Saloon. Too much stress. You know, everyone's such a cokehead in the bars, so it's hard to deal with. I prefer a mellow situation, so I work folding clothes," I said, watching Martha's peaked interest.

"I don't know anything about retail."

"Oh, no. I work at the laundromat. Cool boss and pay is okay. She lets us off a little early sometimes," I added, trying to sound as disinterested as possible. "It's not like a real laundry. It's the Nantucket Laundromat."

"Do you think she's hiring anyone? I need a job. I came because my boyfriend's here," said Martha.

"I'll ask," I generously offered. I rambled on about the tourist economy, the antagonism between Island locals and summer residents, and Nantucket City Council meetings on zoning. I painted an image of politics and drama, obfuscation pieced together to imply that employment was scarce and difficult to obtain. "This is a highly educated work force. Quite ironic, but a good exercise in Marxist principles that would otherwise escape the realities of these college kids."

"I totally agree," said Martha. *Agreeable Martha. How irritating.*

"Come in and fill out an application. When I quit, I'll put in a good word for you."

"Cool. That would be great. Do you know Ted Barrett?"

"Vaguely. I think he's done his laundry there before." My stomach dropped. *Ted and Martha.* I felt queasy. I imagined telling her the truth and her angry confrontation with Ted, and rolled the secret back and forth in my mind like a cinnamon candy on my tongue, sweet and hot.

Her perfume stamped her presence. After she left my head hurt, but I wasn't sure if it was her scent or my imagination. A week later I spied Martha and Ted in front of the coffee shop window. Ted's arm was around her, and he was touching her hair the same way he had touched mine.

I was angry when I came back to my apartment. The phone rang and it was my mother asking me to take a family trip to see Michael. I said no, but when she called again the following week, I decided to go. Helen said she knew she couldn't keep me forever, and I told her a girl named Martha would be coming in. Simple Edie said that she learned some unusual facts listening to my perspectives, and Friendly Felicia asked if I was coming back the next summer. I lied and said I would and Helen said a job was always open.

I was downtown when a man from the group who had called me names in the bar crossed the street to speak to me. I met his eyes with a mean squint and a grimace.

"What," I said flatly. *The enemy.* I was ready to roll. *Stand tall. Stand fierce.*

"I want you to know it wasn't me who said all of that shit. Those other guys, I hardly know them. My girlfriend's Filipino. I think you're all beautiful."

"Your friends are fucking losers. Bunch of assholes," I said dryly, hands on my hips, foot poised ready to kick him in the groin.

"They're not my friends. Sorry about those fuckers. Coming back next year?"

"Maybe."

I stayed an extra week and spent my days letting the rays paint my skin a deep brown, biking past the cranberry bogs in Sconset, and watching the orange sun melt into the blue aluminum waves of Madaket Beach.

I ran into Ted at the grocery store loading up on beer for a party. "Dad and wifey are on Island. A barbeque at the house," said Ted.

"Guess it's all worked out with your Dad and Martha and—"

"You know, some things are better left unsaid." We stood looking at each other as my eyes grew heavy, slowly filling with a warm liquid. My nose clogged up. My ears felt hot, and I wanted to say something but my mouth was dry. I can only remember how I desperately wanted to jump in the freezer, lose myself in frozen pizzas, cans of juice, and boxes of popsicles. I opened the glass door and let a cloud of cool air hit my face. It didn't hide me. "This is lunch. Caterers coming tonight. See ya," he said, filling his cart.

I went home and wadded up his boxer shorts I had been wearing around the apartment and used them to dust off my dresser before throwing them in the broom closet. I called Nick and he came by in his truck. I slept with him figuring that because he was going back to school in California, it'd be a long time, if ever, before I saw him again. The next day he bought me an ice cream cone and we went sailing on a little boat and talked and laughed all day long. As we headed into town that night for a bite to eat, I found myself wistful about leaving.

"I've had a good summer," I said.

"Me, too. But after two years, I'm ready to get back to California," said Nick.

"Do you think you'll come back?"

"It's been good but the summers are too crowded. Winter is nice. Reading. Fishing. Cheap rent. My ex-girlfriend bailed though, got island fever."

"Where's she now?"

"Back in Berkeley living with another guy. What about you?" asked Nick.

"Oh, you know, *Disneyland.*" It was the first time I had used the summer workers' term for Nantucket, slang for the island's alleged reputation as a site of adult hedonistic pleasure. I said it as if to say so would make it true.

I biked by the laundromat three days later and through the window saw Martha folding clothes and Simple Edie sweeping. *The Laundry Ladies.*

That night, I met Nick at the Royal Saloon for a drink and chuckled with the manager; after a few drinks, memories of the restaurant at 10:00 a.m. opening and the stench of garbage and spilt alcohol had faded to an old-fashioned grainy home movie. I spotted Martha and Ted from the corner of my eye.

"I got the job. Thanks for the mention. Ted, do you know Lydia?" asked Martha.

"Hi, Ted. I think we met earlier in the summer," I said coyly.

"We might have, probably not though," said Ted uncomfortably. I looked defiantly into his eyes and he turned away, taking his hand off Martha's shoulder.

"I'm pretty easy to spot here, so probably not if you don't remember," I laughed in agreement. "Maybe I just saw you doing laundry. This is Nick," I said giving Nick a pat on his chest. Nick gave his usual affable grin and I grabbed his arm.

At the end of the evening I kissed Nick a polite good-bye and lied, telling him I had my period, my excuse for not spending the night. He was leaving for the Cape on an early boat to see friends and invited me to go, but I declined.

I was also leaving the next day, on the last boat out. Mom had called crying on the phone; the family trip was cancelled. Michael was going with Stacey to Jamaica. I left a note with my address and phone number in Nick's mailbox and packed my backpack, cleaned out the apartment, and took Ted's silk boxer shorts along with a few old clothes down to the laundromat.

Martha walked over to a washer as it lurched to a stop. "Can you do this for me? There's some nice stuff. Silk's washable. It'd be great if you could fold," I said.

"Sure," said Martha taking the small plastic bag of laundry.

"Thanks," I said smiling.

Wash, dry and fold. I took the numbered chit she handed me, biked down to the wharf, and put the chit in an envelope addressed to Ted with no return address. I anticipated how everything would unravel, how he would tell her about his summer, about me. I did not understand the prevaricating truths between lovers, or how passion is by nature a harbor both reckless and unforgiving. I wanted to be honest and as I biked away I felt a tremendous relief and a feeling of both guarded and wounded pride. Summer over, I sold my bike at the cycle shop, bought a ticket with the cash in my pocket and sat on a bench where I looked out at the murmuring forbidden water and waited for the four o'clock ferry to Cape Cod.

I turned to look one last time at the clean white clapboard houses and saw Ted strolling down the main drag. I faced the ocean as my heart raced and my knee began to bounce up and down. I gripped the seat, felt the rough ridges of wood, and wished for a splinter. Salt inched its way up my nostrils. Ted waved, I pretended not to notice.

"Lydia, going off Island for awhile?"

"Yeah," I said looking at the ground. I felt the heat rise off my face and my body stiffen as my stomach wound into a tight acid knot.

"I'm going to tell Martha about stuff, but I haven't yet," he said quietly.

"I know." The ferry was pulling into the harbor and I could see the indecipherable blobs of light and dark, people strolling along the decks, lifting and dropping their bags, and calling out to each other. Ted looked at my backpack.

"I thought you'd be cool about it," said Ted awkwardly.

I took a step back and started towards the ferry. A voice rose from my throat; it was laughing, shouting, and sobbing, but eerily nothing came out. I was cutting through the water and swimming miles past the dock.

"I love you, bye," I said simply.

I love you, too.

I caught them. Astonished blue eyes. Everything sharp and bitter. No theme song, just the sound of the water and a dull pain gnawing at my heart. I picked up my bags and ran down to the ferry, hoping that maybe he would run after me, wanting him to say something, but knowing that he wouldn't, and wishing with all of my body that I'd never see him again.

I never did.

LANGUAGES

September 21

Once again, I am without prospects.

"The problem with last week's meeting was that Mr. Bhang met a potential wife the week prior through another matchmaker," said Mrs. Park over the phone. "Of course, Miss Lee, I had no idea he would use another matchmaker. But don't worry, that sort of man is bound to be an unreliable husband. If he can't be loyal to a matchmaker, why would he be loyal to a wife?" She said this in a flustered voice. Her logic made sense, but it is no matter, as today Mother said she would not pay for any more introductions; the next time I will be responsible for the fee. I will have to wait until next month's paycheck.

I cannot decide if each meeting makes for better practice, or if it leaves me feeling more discouraged. I say to Mrs. Park that I have full faith in her services, and tell Mother I will meet the right man and marry soon, but I feel insecure. I have no right to complain about any introduction and cannot reject a candidate without suffering the humiliation of Mother's words: "You'll never marry. You're thirty-two years old!"

I find it all very tiresome.

With the exception of Mr. Chung, all of the men whom I have been introduced to are single for the very good reason that no one wants them! They are too old, too unattractive, have mothers who are unbearably involved in their lives, or have weaknesses for drinking or gambling. There is no one decent left.

The one man I did like, Mr. Chung, said to Mrs. Park, "My mother feels that Miss Lee is a little too tall." I am approximately 5'8". I am told his mother also said my teeth were too crooked. Unfortunately, I did find myself smiling a great deal during my meeting with Mr. Chung, and so my teeth were therefore noticeable. Regardless, he left for the United

States over a year ago—with another more suitable wife. Someone no doubt, who does not have crooked teeth, or at the very least, has the sense not to smile so widely.

I am trying not to show my worries about my unmarried state as I feel that to do so is unattractive. I read that one should take up hobbies and activities and that men, if unable to find a beautiful woman, will content themselves with one who will establish a comfortable home and a stimulating academic environment for their children.

That is the reason I gave Mother for my Friday night Italian language class. I have always wanted to travel to Rome and Venice. The people look beautiful and romantic and I adore the garlic bread they serve at the Italian restaurant across from the Lotte Hotel.

Mother disagrees, "The last thing you need is to speak Italian. The reason you're not married is that you study too hard and fill your head with ideas that make you unmarriageable." Maybe she is right. All of my classmates are married. Mother said Father's sixtieth birthday will be a complete disaster unless I am married. "Why, you will be nearly thirty-three! By the time I was twenty-six, I already had both you and Son Ae! Your younger sister is married with two little boys and a rich husband no less." I'm the obstacle to what would otherwise be her perfect life. The fact that she had no sons was frowned upon by both sets of grandparents, but I suppose she no longer remembers what it was like to suffer family disapproval.

Today Mihee sent a letter announcing her plans to marry Keith the Chinese-Australian engineer. She invited me to the wedding but it will be impossible for me to go. Still, I circled the date on my calendar. She won't be returning to Seoul. When she first moved there she said she missed Korea, but about six months ago, her letters changed. *I hope I can find work here. I would like to stay and make a life in Australia. Sometime you have to visit me. Recently, I have met a very nice man…*A harsh reminder of my own dreadful situation. Never mind, I have to prepare tomorrow's lesson.

October 12

But today's class discussion on marriage further confirmed my beliefs about Westerners. Still, my students are open-minded compared to most foreigners, many of whom barely bother to learn anything more than "Thank you" or "How are you?" after living here more than a dozen years!

On the street, I once saw a foreigner scream at a Korean for not knowing how to speak English! Ridiculous. The Westerners' preoccupation with the physical dominates their existence and confounds explanation. Their minds are instruments for their bodies; enslaved by base human desires, they show no restraint. I find it disconcerting. There was much laughter and jocular behavior when the discussion regarding men and women turned to descriptions detailing certain kinds of bodily intimacies.

The entire class laughed when Matthew the American said, "In Korea, boys and boys hold hands. Girls and girls hold hands. But boys hold hands with girls, girls hold hands with boys...cannot!" He shook his head and pretended to pull out his hair. "Strange Koreans," he said.

His spoken Korean is terrible, but his writing is not so bad. He is part of the university's exchange student program in political science. Because of the great effort he puts forward, I think of him as one of my best students. Every morning, I see him playing basketball with our students. They stand much shorter than him. Although American, he is well-mannered and polite. He is 21 years old.

"Hand holding between the same sex is a nice Korean custom," I said. "Why don't boys hold hands in America? They are afraid it is 'gay'—this is silly."

"Very silly. Extremely silly American behavior," said Andrew. Andrew is British and has been an English teacher at a girls' high school. "British too, though, are same." He joked, "Matthew sounds frustrated. Matthew is an American college student."

"I would like to hold hands with a girl. Korean or American. I cannot!" said Matthew.

Sister Takamoto, the elderly Japanese nun, quietly listens during those discussions about men and women and said, "Matthew must be patient." This too made the class laugh because she so far has refrained from any disapproving comment. The students enjoy her presence very much. After finishing the language course she will go to work at an orphanage in Kwang Ju.

Every day for the past two weeks, Matthew has carried my tape recorder for dictations to the office. Andrew said, "Matthew is the most attentive student I've ever seen."

"Korean conversation practice," said Matthew. Then he hit Andrew on the shoulder. The two students are very good friends and they are always joking with each other.

This afternoon Mrs. Park called and said that she would do her best to see that I had proper introductions within the coming months. "Don't worry. Worrying makes frown lines which no woman needs. We'll have you married off by the time your father celebrates his birthday. There is a right man out there for you. I will catch one for you with my good hunting technique," she said. It was reassuring to speak with her.

October 19

I have taught long enough to know that there is always a student who may harbor a secret liking for the teacher. The student mistakes the act of teaching for true affection. This harmless behavior usually lasts until the first test, at which point the student realizes that the teacher is not only teaching him, but a classroom of students, and that no special favors will be granted.

I am certain that the Korean girls look at Matthew. He is tall, and has the kind of appearance seen in American magazines and movies. Other teachers have said that Matthew is rather handsome. I am not in disagreement, but unlike Miss Choo, who vocalizes her opinions and relishes gossip about the students, it is not my style to notice or comment upon students' physical characteristics.

Three days ago, Matthew presented me with an apple and explained the Western custom of bringing apples to teachers. The class teased him and called him a "teacher's pet." But I corrected them, "I assure you all that Matthew will not receive any special points. In Korea, we have a fair system of grading." I took a bite out of the apple.

October 29

Westerners have an insistent nature. For two days we have discussed age relationships in class. Matthew asked if we could be friends despite our age difference. I said, "In Korean society, disparate ages prohibit a proper relationship on equal footing between two people like us, who may have a gap of eleven years between them. The older one will always be accorded the respect of age and wisdom."

"I agree," said Matthew.

"There will always be a slight, but detectable deference to age on the part of the younger person in the relationship," I said. He said that in the West it is often the same. I disagreed, "Really, in Korea, it is different."

He smiled as I said this; then put his head down to concentrate on his paper. Sister Takamoto added that in Japan too, respect was given to the older person. Andrew said that Americans in particular had a tendency to worship the young.

I was glad when class ended. Sometimes Matthew is so very forward. I can't tell if he is serious. I myself am a serious person and there are people who don't understand this.

Mother showed me the guest list that she is making for father's party and we discussed the kinds of food that will be served. Since so many people are coming, mother wants to make a good impression and may also serve Western food in addition to Korean food. But my father really does not like Western food, so this may change.

On Friday, I received a picture of Mihee and her fiancée Keith. They were sitting at a café holding hands and smiling. Behind them sparkled the blue ocean. They looked happy together. He is nice looking with a tan face and elegant nose. Not too flat, not too big. Mihee wrote a note on the inside of a card featuring a surfer and said that Keith likes outdoor sports. They are learning how to scuba dive! I cannot picture Mihee doing such a thing, although I do remember that she liked to swim. They go hiking together. Chinese Australians must like to hike as much as we Koreans do.

I remember one junior high hiking excursion to Mount Sorak with Mihee. We wandered off the trail together away from the rest of the class and she shared with me the special candy she brought. Real Belgian chocolate from her father's business acquaintance. Delicious. It was the only time I was ever in trouble at school. When we ran to catch up with the rest of the class, the teacher made us go to the end of the line together. The next morning we had to help clean the floor of the school, but every time the teacher turned around we smiled at each other. We were naughty, but Mihee made it seem fun.

October 30

Matthew wore a red wool sweater today. Underneath he wore a blue T-shirt in that disheveled American style. When he took his sweater off before class started, his shirt came up and I noticed that he had some hair in a line on his muscular stomach. Muscles can be overwhelming and not so attractive. This must be unfortunate for him though I suppose some women find this style of body handsome. His ears stick out a little too much. Father says that means such a person is a good listener. Matthew is an excellent listener, although his Korean accent is still terrible.

He told the class that over the weekend, he moved to another boarding house due to difficulty with the woman, the landlord (landlady?). Students have a terrible lot. They are often victims of stingy proprietors who shut off their heat, or give them too small portions of food for breakfast. If the student complains, landlords say that they are ungrateful! A foreign student may be derided as an example of the decadent and immoral West.

Matthew carried my tape recorder to the office and I found myself walking slowly, letting him practice speaking Korean. "My Korean language is not improving fast," he said.

"Why?" I asked him.

"On the weekend I went to Grace Department Store for shopping—a pager. Koreans did not understand me."

"What happened?"

"I ask, pager okay in USA? Okay Australia? My Korean is bad. The salesman. No help. Another salesman came. Asking. Another salesman came. All try to speak Korean. Seven salesmen try help me. Laugh! Laugh many!" said Matthew in Korean.

I laughed out loud, my mouth wide open. "Cute teeth," said Matthew. I closed my mouth and smiled with my lips closed.

"Nice teeth, beautiful teeth?" he said in Korean. Then in English he said, "Oh god, I mean—" he corrected himself and said in Korean, "How do you say? Oh, nice mouth, nice smile." Then, he asked in English, "Now, you said before we are unable to fraternize due to our age difference, correct?"

"Yes, I am glad you were listening," I said in Korean. "In Korea, speak Korean please."

"Ah!" groaned Matthew. "Okay. Question. Korean. Not English. Okay?"

"Okay," I said.

"Maybe coffee to meet to discuss Korean grammar? I am a student. I am thank you for luck. You are teacher. I like Korean studies." His face went deep pink.

"Yes, it is possible. Sometimes it happens; sometime we can meet," I answered in Korean. "No problem," I said in English. I am flattered that he thinks highly of me in this way. I do try my best to be a good teacher.

November 5

Mother said she will pay for two more meetings before Father's sixtieth birthday. It doesn't seem likely that any man will marry me before. Mrs. Park is trying to arrange a meeting with Mr. Sun, a divorced dentist with a four-year-old daughter. He briefly studied overseas in the U.S. What about the mother? What type of man gets a divorce when he has a small child? I know there are many divorces these days. Mother expressed her hesitancy about this issue to Mrs. Park. But when I said that Mr. Sun was not an ideal candidate, Mother said, "Who wants to raise another woman's child? Who wants a divorced man? But time is running out!" I shall meet Mr. Sun.

When I walk down the street by Ewha Woman's University and see shop after shop of wedding dresses, wedding photography studios, anything and everything necessary for a wedding, I feel terribly alone. The huge painted billboard advertisement in the middle of the Shinchon center of the young bride and groom, the couples in the palace gardens posing in their wedding regalia—it's all very disheartening. If I allow myself to think about my future, I try to think like a modern woman. I am a modern woman. But are couples really that happy? My married friends complain that their husbands stay out late. Or they have mother-in-law problems. But this must be better than single life.

I went to Myeongdong Cathedral on Sunday for Mass. The church is crowded these days, yet I find the new priest's sermons dull. I went to confession. I walked past the church and down the block to the restaurant where I went with others from youth fellowship five, ten years ago.

The streets wind along and the smells of the steaming food from the restaurants invite the passerby to enter for a bowl of steaming *mandu* afloat in a broth with slivers of green. I strolled by the little stand of the cobbler who once fixed the heels of my shoes. His window was shut. I remember staring at his black nails and dirty hands and thinking how the stains never went away, how he would probably die with those stains, be buried with those stains on his hands. Whenever I see the uniformed high school students carrying their backpacks, I am pulled back to those days long ago.

I see a few of the youth fellowship friends at Mass. Others do not come as regularly, or have moved away. They may live in Seoul, but we meet infrequently. Most are married. When I was younger, I wanted the future to come. Now it is here. It is not how I thought it would be.

Matthew has been sick. He showed up on Monday coughing and looking dreadful. He didn't come the rest of the week and may even be out for another few days into the next. Andrew has taken the work to him though I doubt he will do much of it due to his poor condition. Without Matthew class has been quiet. Even Andrew is not talking as much as he usually does.

I didn't go to Italian class and came home early. Father's birthday celebration is a good excuse for Mother and Uncle to fight. They have always argued. He was visiting and within minutes of me walking into the house he started asking me about my marriage prospects. Of course, I just said that I have not yet met the right person. He nodded and left shortly afterwards.

My mother looked haggard, her mouth pinched into a tight screw like she had eaten something sour. "You're getting older. Why can't you find someone? Don't you know how difficult this is? Do you want to be alone? Everything I do and still you are not married!" Mother yelled.

Uncle apparently said that I would never get married and that I am withering away like an old maid. This enraged Mother; she took her anger out on me, recounting every insult Uncle made. I am so tired. I look in the mirror and see spider lines around my eyes. Time spins everything. I fade away.

November 12

Matthew came back today. He looked tired and weak, but claimed that he was fully recovered. He asked for special permission to drink orange juice during class. He looked so ill that I recanted my previous rule. He said, "The Korean cold is more deadly than the American cold. Tell me, are the women this deadly?" This type of nonsense talk about Korea usually makes me mad, but I realized he was trying to tell a joke. Also, I have heard him say he thinks Korean women are beautiful. But it was not funny. Maybe he was sick.

He looks thinner. I told him he needed to eat more for his strength. His mother sent him some special food from home—favorite breakfast cereals, cookies, vitamins—he cannot cook at a boarding house. He told the class about his single disastrous attempt to cook Korean food at a friend's house. "Everywhere bad taste. Tasting like bad food! I'm a bad cook! All food turn black! Fire! Fire!" The class laughed at his movements and his re-enactment of his bad cooking. He eats Korean food, but says that he cannot stomach spicy food. Andrew says he loves spicy food, but only since he's been in Korea.

I've been extremely busy organizing the curriculum for next year. Italian class goes well. They may have a tour group to Italy through the language program at the university. Who knows if it will happen, or if I will even have enough money to go.

December 5

Sister Takamoto brought Matthew a hat she knitted for him. It is dark blue with white trim and Matthew was pleased and touched. "Now you can be warm," said Sister Takamoto with a serene smile. She is like a kind grandmother. Matthew wore the hat during class.

Mr. Chung returned from America much sooner than he expected. Mrs. Park told me that his pregnant wife didn't want to have her baby away from her family. When I went to Mrs. Park's apartment two days ago, I saw the wedding picture of Mr. Chung and his bride. She is a very beautiful twenty-five-year-old. Her teeth are small and even. White. Her eyes are round and wide from surgery.

Mother tried to make me have my eyelids fixed, like everyone else during college over winter vacation of freshman year, but I was too afraid. All the models and actresses in Korea have surgery. I should not have been scared. Eyes are more glamorous and beautiful after surgery, but I still don't have the courage to be beautiful. My eyes are small; I have single lids.

I saw my friend Hisoo's eyes the day after her surgery. The sight of the black and blue skin and sutures made me feel sick. For a long time afterwards, I would see the knife slit scar on her eyelids and feel queasy. Months later, though it properly healed, when I looked at her, I would only see a shadowed image of the mangled lid and puffy skin around her eyes. Hisoo's mother said that it would improve Hisoo's looks, and thus her marriage choices. Shortly after her scars healed, Hisoo met a man from a good family. She's pretty. They have two beautiful children and a nice apartment in Apgujeong with a view of the Han River.

Mr. Sun was a disappointment. He was tall and at first polite, but then asked my opinions on parenting. He only discussed his daughter. I am sure he wants someone who will be a good mother, but he insisted on speaking to me in English and said he would like his child to also speak English. He said one of the reasons he agreed to meet me was because I could speak English in the house, a skill his daughter could then acquire. He asked if I was a good cook. It was uncomfortable. Mrs. Park kept trying to soften his remarks and said, "Miss Lee is an excellent English teacher. A perfect mother for any child." Given the circumstances, I did not necessarily expect a good meeting, but I felt discouraged about marriage. No choices.

January 5

I am so grateful that today is Friday because I embarrassed myself in front of Matthew and Andrew.

I was walking down the hall as usual, and studying the tips of my Italian shoes. They are extremely uncomfortable, but I like to wear them. They cost so much money. I looked up and became aware of Matthew staring. For some reason, it embarrassed me. Something about the way he looked. Heat rose off my face. I eased myself into his eyes; I really could not control myself.

I walked slowly, aware of the smooth lining of my skirt brushing against my thigh. My shoes pinched the top of my biggest toe. This often happens when I stop suddenly and fast on bumpy pavement or when I run up the steps from the subway. I felt the tag of my shirt chafing against the back of my neck; I could not bother to reach it. I moved my shoulder to alleviate the irritation. Color in my cheeks.

I failed to notice where, in the classroom doorway, the wall sticks out. We were looking at each other and then I bumped my head!

I recovered by scurrying off into the classroom. Oh, I do not know why I did not notice the wall; I simply did not see it. How mortifying!

I could feel Matthew's surreptitious smile. Muffled laughter from Andrew. From the sound and intonation of Matthew's voice, he was protesting whatever Andrew was saying. I hope no one else saw it.

After class, Matthew carried my tape recorder. He was rather forward. He asked me about my weekend free time. I said I was busy. The pitch of his voice was higher. I found it difficult to meet his eye. Relief when he went on to class.

January 15

Today I went to buy Mihee's wedding gift at the Lotte Department Store, a set of dessert silverware. They are the kind that I would like to have if someone gave me a wedding gift, if I have a wedding. I spent much more money than I planned, which decidedly eliminates the possibility of having any matchmaker meetings other than the appointments Mother paid for. I hope Mihee likes it.

Today I found out that Matthew may have a girlfriend! I can't believe it.

A third-generation Korean Russian—Tatiana. I heard that she is a good student and the daughter of a Moscow University professor and a violinist. She is beautiful and approximately twenty-three or twenty-four years old. I watched them walk out the door to lunch this afternoon and noticed how their bodies were close to each other, no space between them. He touched her arm and waist in an intimate, almost inappropriate way. Tatiana turned to look up at Matthew and laughed. Her dyed brown hair is longer than mine and her clothes are fashionable and expensive. Her skirts are long and tight. I feel she is really not a nice student, though Miss Choo says Tatiana does study hard. It is difficult to believe.

When Matthew carried my tape recorder to class, I found myself trying to engage him in conversation. He was distracted. The level of attentiveness he demonstrated in the past was not there. Maybe he is not really a reliable type of person. When he rolled up his sleeves today I noticed a great deal of hair on his arms. Also, some veins probably from exercising too much. Tatiana must notice these things, but she probably doesn't think about it.

January 23

Andrew brought strange music to class: Gregorian chants. Sister Takamoto wasn't familiar with these particular chants but knew what they were. Andrew said they were an early form of Western classical music, if not the earliest form. Matthew said he liked all music, but said that Gregorian chants were not pleasant to the ear. Sister Takamoto smiled and said that although she was a nun, she would have to agree about the sound of Gregorian chants. Everyone laughed.

Matthew has been friendly, but I feel anxious lately. I want to be a good teacher, but I've been thinking about my father, about the matchmaker, and it's been difficult to stop these thoughts.

Mother has been talking about father's birthday plans, and has discussed giving him a long vacation as a present. Maybe they will go overseas for a holiday to Hawaii. These days I have been trying to avoid too much discussion about his birthday because I know what she will say about my future and marriage.

January 28

Today I overheard Matthew: "The last thing I need is a self-obsessed girlfriend whose main preoccupation in life are idiotic American GI's in Itaewon." Miss Choo said that's what Tatiana and her two friends do on the weekend. I'm surprised; then again, she's a foreign-born Korean, and even those from nice families display this kind of unthinkable behavior in Seoul.

When Matthew carried my tape recorder, he said in English, "This term has changed my academic and philosophic perceptions of Korea."

"How have you changed?" I asked in Korean. He nodded his head and switched to Korean.

"Well, I'm not sure if I've changed. I think I'm just understanding more."

"Your language is much better. It's improved a tremendous amount," I said.

"Not just the language," he pointed to his forehead. "Thinking. I understand the thinking more."

"Good. I am glad to hear that. How do you find Korea now?"

"Interesting. Different. Surprising. In a good way, of course. I like your dress," he said.

It is the slightest amount shorter than my usual skirt length. I know that since the skirt is tight around my hips Matthew would notice and say something, but I wore it because most of my other clothes are at the cleaners. I used to feel irritated or embarrassed when the salary men on the subway would look at me in this dress, so I haven't worn it in a long time. I hope Matthew doesn't think my skirt is tight like Tatiana's skirts. I don't know. I must be a crazy woman! Maybe he is noticing things because Tatiana is not around. He did not shave today. I hope he is not growing a beard. He looks very messy and I heard he sometimes goes out drinking with Andrew and other students. Then he said in Korean, "The dress is a nice color on you."

I said, "Thank you." I could feel his eyes travel up the back of my legs and carefully climb up my spine and rest on the nape of my neck. My hair was up. I turned towards him, away from the chalkboard. He pretended to be in the middle of reading an important passage of his book. I wore perfume. Matthew the American.

February 6

Matthew is not with Tatiana anymore. Her teacher, Mrs. Yu, told Miss Choo, who spread the news today in the teacher's office. Tatiana is too young to appreciate Matthew's youthful curiosity. This type of charm is lost on a young woman. Her type seeks out the company of those who are older. She probably looks for the qualities I would find offensive. A younger person finds flaws and bad habits exciting, a sign of wisdom or experience.

Again, he did not shave. He is not growing a beard, but he sometimes does not shave in the morning before school. I'm not sure why. I think this is that new American style, but I don't find it attractive. Andrew made a joke about Matthew and said Matthew is trying to look like an American rock star. Matthew said he was trying to be a British pop star, not an American rock star.

Maybe there are cultural differences between Matthew and Tatiana. They are Western, but she is Russian. And Korean. Americans and Russians are very different.

Hisoo called me. We have not spoken in some months now. She urged me to come by her apartment and said we must get together, talk about old times and catch up on each other's lives. She said she would find out about a man she heard her cousin decided not to marry. She said this man was nice, and that her cousin is bossy and the kind who would drive any good man away. I'm not too excited about this, but agreed to meet this man if Hisoo could arrange it.

February 13

Sister Takamoto gave me a lovely pair of knitted mittens. I haven't worn mittens since I was a child, and prefer to wear gloves, but these are beautifully knit. They are a peach color and it matches a scarf she has seen me wear. Matthew wears the hat that she knitted him every day. He said, "Those are beautiful mittens. And they look very nice." I smiled and so did Sister Takamoto.

In the past I have ignored the overtures made by Western men. In general, I find their hairy bodies and demeanor not to my liking. Matthew is different, free from the vortex of his society, avoiding its vacuum by journeying here to the East. If I were younger, I would surely find him attractive. Maybe I would brave romance. Maybe we would fall in love and live in the U.S. Maybe we would even have a swimming pool surrounded by a garden of red roses. Our children would be wide eyed. I'm sure if I was a younger, more adventurous woman I would probably find Matthew interesting. He's very young, but even if he was older, he is not the kind of man I could see myself really marrying.

Besides, I never want to leave Korea. Westerners don't understand Koreans.

Mother said, "Your father and I won't be here forever. What will happen to you after we are gone? Who will take care of you?" Today she bought me a scarf. We talked about father's birthday. She said, "I'm sure it will be a great celebration. I want to thank you for helping me so much. You're a good daughter." It made me sad to hear this.

February 20

For my matchmaker meeting I wore the beige dress I wore three years ago at my very first meeting with Mrs. Park, along with my new scarf. "There is some issue or concern on the part of this man regarding your height. Mr. Kim is less than one inch taller than you are."

"I usually wear flat shoes," I said.

"True. And you look very nice," said Mrs. Park. "He should feel lucky. Tall children come from a tall mother."

I smiled but did not say anything. Koreans say they like tall women, but they always tell me I'm too tall. I used to get upset. Now I just don't care. It is always something: too tall, too slender, bad teeth, too studious, too quiet, too talkative, and always, they say that I am too Westernized. They worry I will not behave as expected and that I will get strange ideas from teaching foreigners.

When Mr. Kim walked into the room, my heart sank. He has a moustache! I don't know why. This is not Korean. Mrs. Park told me that

Mr. Kim, an art professor, studied art history in Paris, France, and had many unique foreign experiences and has foreign friends. He is almost fifty, portly and nearly bald. He was interested in my Italian lessons and visited Italy twenty years ago. He talked about Michelangelo and the Sistine Chapel. We drank tea and ate cookies, and then he said he had to be going to another engagement, but that he had a pleasant time. He was kind, but I don't want to marry a man who is almost twenty years older than I am with a moustache! This man, or a man like him, may well be my future. But I don't want to marry avuncular Mr. Kim. Help!

Mrs. Park saw my crestfallen face and said, "I'm sure with the right persuasion, he would shave his moustache. He would be handsome without it!" I did not respond. "Mr. Kim may not seem like the kind of man you would pick out to be your husband, but I know. All of these years of matchmaking, I know what makes a good husband. He is old enough to treat you well and would treasure you."

"He seemed nice," was all I could say. "I liked hearing about his travels."

"Maybe one day he will take you to Europe," said Mrs. Park. "How many married men are there who would travel with their wives like that? He is a good man. Think about this," she said finally.

"I will think about it," I said.

"But don't think too long," she said.

I remain unconvinced.

February 26

This morning I woke up in a sweat. I couldn't remember what I dreamt, but Matthew was in the dream and we were arguing. I must be a crazy woman. I have nothing to argue with him about. Matthew tells funny stories. I laugh around him. Furthermore, I never argue with students. Very strange. When I awoke, I found myself upside down, my head and feet at the opposite sides of the bed.

My entire family is coming for father's sixtieth birthday. Relatives all the way from Busan and one who lives in Hong Kong, so Mother has now reserved a hotel banquet room. Il Young will be presenting my father with a new automobile. Mother says, "Your sister has such a wonderful husband. We're so lucky to have such a son-in-law." She has stopped commenting on the matchmaker meetings.

Mrs. Park said, "Mr. Kim would very much like to see you again. Are you interested?" I agreed after thinking about it for a few days because time is pressing down upon me. A moustache. Fifty years old. Bald. Overweight. Mr. Kim is not how I imagined my future husband. I may see him again, but will refuse the third visit. If I didn't, he would think I wanted to marry him.

Matthew is handsome but I couldn't begin to consider someone like him. He may be good-looking, but he is far too young. I also find a hirsute body unappealing. (I like that word "hirsute" that I recently learned.) The only men I have seen with hair like that on their bodies are in movies. I would only marry a Korean. His Korean is much better these days, but I could never leave Korea. He is too young, too hirsute.

March 9

Today Mihee and Keith were married. Her mother and father flew to Australia. She and Keith will visit Korea next year.

Next spring, the Italian language class is going on a trip to Italy for ten days. They will visit three cities: Rome, Florence and Venice. I will not mention this to Mother.

One more week before school is out. The students are ready for vacation, low concentration these days. Today the class went to the Lotte World amusement park on a field trip. Matthew happened to stand beside me in line for the rollercoaster ride so we rode together. My heart flew when we went up and down and he yelled with great enthusiasm. It was exhilarating. I was completely out of breath; my knees were soft. We were pushed together as we went around the turns. He told me how he loves rollercoaster rides. Andrew and Sister Takamoto rode behind us. I was worried when I looked behind and saw her round shocked eyes, but the sister found it very entertaining and afterwards smiled with great enthusiasm. I am sure it was quite a change in her daily routine of prayer and school. She is extremely good-natured. Afterwards, Andrew graciously offered her a drink of water.

When I came home I went to the public bath. I like soaking in the hot water and the feeling of the bubbles pulsing against my back. I closed my eyes and felt my skin and looked at all of the women. Many different sizes and shapes, old and young—wrinkles, big stomachs, small waists, skinny legs, fat arms. Some are slender, some are round. I wonder what women think about when they first undress for a man. I myself have never been naked in front of a man.

March 15

I saw Matthew at Namdaemun Market.

I went to find some clothes for my nephews and there was Matthew with his hands in his pockets, wearing his hat, walking between old women hawking their food, vendors bickering with customers—he seemed almost lost in the pile of goods falling and spilling into the street.

The market fills me with a sense of pride and belonging. Mother hates the market and only goes there if she has no choice. She prefers the control of the department store. I'm more old-fashioned. The swarm of people and their frenzied action makes me feel oddly content. I have come here since I was a child and I shall go here my entire life. Satisfaction in consistency. I may complain or tire of it, but all worlds, in one respect, must be the same. We are tiny and insignificant, hence our joy should be found in whatever way possible. I believe this, but I am impatient.

Matthew looked happy. I greeted him and asked him about the rest of his holiday. "I'd made plans to travel to Thailand, but decided to postpone the visit until the end of next term," he said in English. Then in Korean he asked, "How is your vacation going?"

"I am preparing for my father's birthday celebration. The sixtieth birthday is very important for Koreans," I replied in Korean.

"Yes, I know," he said. "Are you planning a big party?"

"Yes, of course, with many relatives visiting."

"Would you like to get some lunch together?" he asked. I felt like immediately saying yes, but I showed some reluctance to eat with him.

"I must be going home. I am very busy."

"Please stay. I need to buy you lunch in thanks for all of your teaching," he insisted. As we spoke we switched back and forth between Korean and English. He asked again in Korean, then in English. I finally relented. "Fantastic. Where's a good place to go around here?"

I enjoyed lunch. I laughed out loud at least three times. My teeth showed. I didn't care. He asked about my family and said his new landlady was slightly better than the one before, but not by much. He talked about his boarding house and traveling to Thailand. I think of someone like Matthew and what he will do, and the unknown woman he will marry, and I think that I too, held dreams of escape, of travel, of love, of something different.

Recently, a Westerner told me that he was glad to leave Korea, as he felt that there were no dreams here. I disagree. We simply guard them close to our bodies. Dreams are private and fragile. I have dreams; still, it remains difficult for them to surface and swim in the open. Now and then I search out other dreams. If I find any, I quickly sequester them. They are in languages unable to be translated. *Koom chaj kee ohrop da.* Misinterpreted or lost, lodged in labyrinths or wells. I try to keep them out of the sun; they balance on the tip of my tongue, they render me mute. I waken from my reverie—I am too old. I should stop.

I bought Father a golf club. It is the kind he wants but has been unable to justify its price to Mother. When I showed her the club she said, "The best thing you could give your father is a marriage to a suitable man."

I found myself telling Matthew all of this over lunch. I told him of the difficulty of finding a husband. I am too loquacious. He was surprised to learn I did not have a boyfriend. He expressed sympathy for my plight. I found it awkward so I said in Korean, "How is Tatiana?" He was surprised, and waved his hand and laughed.

"Not my type of woman," he said.

"What's your type?"

"Definitely not the Tatiana type," he said. We discussed in delicate terms the differences of culture, personality, and age that may prohibit a love or even enhance desire. Korean and English. English and Korean. He seemed comfortable in both languages.

"It's difficult to meet the right person. But I am a choosey person. Very hard to get along with."

"I don't see that," said Matthew. "I think everyone has a hard time, really," he said in Korean. "I think who you love is always a surprise; sometimes you think you want someone because outside, it seems like you are alike, but you find the person is very different inside."

"You sound very experienced," I said in English. "I am older than you but not experienced."

"You are probably experienced in other ways, that's all," said Matthew. I have never talked like this to a man. He said in the West, love was spontaneity and surprise, impulse and desire, something which people could not, or did not control. "I fell in love once. But it didn't work out," he admitted.

"Were you going to marry?"

"Marriage? It's hard to say, but I did feel strongly for her. I loved her."

"You must be lonely," I said in Korean.

"I am. But I feel differently now. I want experience. Love and wisdom. I don't think you can plan love. I'm not sure if that's American, or me," he said.

He explained how love can be momentary or lengthy, but above all is unable to be strictly defined. Giddiness. I think I was saying too much. I felt nervous when I first looked at him, but then I relaxed. He is easy to talk to.

We left the coffee shop, he folded his umbrella up under his arm. After I made a joke about the American style of doing things, he gently hit my bottom with the top of his umbrella! I was startled, but I giggled. He grinned. I could feel my body temperature rise. It started to lightly rain, the drops cooled my face. He opened his umbrella and ushered me under it like a child. Our shoulders bumped. First he apologized, and then he said, "No, I'm not sorry for that at all, I want my shoulder to touch yours." I tried to focus on the wall and realized that we were in the alley alone.

I saw a stooped old grandfather dressed in a hanbok; the deep blue silk vest and shiny gray stiff pants, the white-white thin collar in a neatly sharpened "V." He walked with a cane. His face was frail and crumpled. I thought of how odd I must look to him, how shameful, how modern, but he did not notice us. Matthew turned to me and moved closer and bent down still holding the umbrella, though by now, most of the rain stopped. He used it as a shield, and took my packages and placed them under his arm. He kissed me.

His lips gently grazed over mine, and I could scarcely feel him. Then he kissed me again. I hesitated, then imitated him, growing smaller as his embrace grew larger, until I too, filled the space. I held on, not wanting to let go, everything disappearing and emerging. We kept kissing a long time. It was probably only for seconds, but it felt much longer. Sheltered by his body, sinking deep into him, I felt hopeful. Clean. All geography and time fell away.

I managed to say farewell and return home, running and out of breath by the time I reached the door. I went to my room and laughed and cried alone. I write this down to save it.

March 31

I will see Matthew next Saturday. I am excited. I think about him all the time. It makes no sense, but then again, it does. I looked through my closet and afterwards went shopping for new clothes two times this week. I wonder what Matthew thinks about Italy. *Sa rahng hey yo.* I love you. It's crazy. Mother's in a good mood as Son Ae has come up to help prepare for Father's birthday and brought her two children. Son Ae says I look unusually well and when she asked if I had any future marriage prospects I told her about Mr. Kim. I have to call Mrs. Park to arrange the second meeting with Mr. Kim. Then, Son Ae confided to me in tears, making me promise that I would not tell Mother—that lousy husband Il Young has a mistress! Son Ae cried and cried. She said an older man like Mr. Kim would surely not do such a thing to a young wife. This still does not endear Mr. Kim to me.

I was tempted to tell Son Ae about Matthew. I need to go to confession. I do care. I don't care. I look in the mirror and smile. My teeth are not so terrible. I fantasize about America. No promise, no expectations. I have feelings of happiness.

MY FRIEND FAITH, 1977

We agreed to exchange gifts. Faith spent the last few weeks before I left Seoul showing me the jewelry she would like to buy if she had the money, or receive as a gift from her parents, or a friend, if she had a friend in Korea, but we both knew I was her only friend other than Miss Hong, her helper, and since it wasn't Faith's birthday or Christmas, it was unlikely that Miss Hong would buy her a present.

I thought Faith rude for her audacity, but did not tell her so.

Faith window-shopped as I spent the cash my relatives had given me on presents for family and friends back home. Our tastes were different: she liked dangly earrings with flowers and baubles, and I preferred posts with small stones, but it didn't matter, she reassured me, she would never ever be picky about a present.

Like me, Faith was twelve years old, born in the U.S., and her family's eldest child. Unlike me, she was the long red-haired daughter of Baptist missionaries from Georgia, fully developed, and was home schooled by her mother. My black bowl cut, gangly limbs, and flat chest caused me to be frequently mistaken for a boy. I sported gold wire rims with thick plastic lenses, and attended Pine Cove Junior High in a small California town by the same name.

Faith had lived in Seoul since she was five and spoke fluent Korean. Like my Hawaiian-born Korean mother, I understood only rudimentary Korean used to enforce discipline and describe bodily functions: *Ahn-juh*. Sit down. *Chin-chi chap su say yo.* Come and eat. *Cho young i heh.* Be quiet. *Pahn-goo.* Fart. Faith's family prayed at mealtime, forbid her from wearing shorts, and stressed to her the importance of being a nice young lady. We did not pray, I preferred jeans to skirts, and my parents' concerns were not so much that I understand the feminine virtues of docility and grace, but that I proudly embrace my Korean heritage. Their goals were neither lofty nor unreasonable, but were incompatible with my own which were to assimilate with my white Christian American peers, a daunting challenge that I naively and stubbornly refused to surrender.

The summer of 1977, my grandfather sent a single round-trip plane ticket to Seoul, an earnest attempt to ensure the proper unfolding of my Korean identity. The adventure was presented, if not disguised as a glorious opportunity, but I told my mother I preferred to spend the summer at home swimming in the Pine Cove pool with my sister Mia, catching fireflies at dusk, biting into thick wedges of watermelon and having seed-spitting contests with the neighborhood kids—drifting through another season where the days lazily eased into each other, unchanged and marked by picnics, the smell of fresh grass and the steady number of mosquito bites on my legs.

"You play with your cousins. Remember Pu Pyung?" said Dad. I was only five the year we lived on the U.S. Army base in Korea and my memories were vague. I thought of my father clad in his military uniform bringing large plastic jugs of clean water home from the base. Then, there was the cold fall night when the family came over to carefully bury the kimchi stored in large ceramic containers. They were put in a large hole dug by my grandfather's chauffeur and were to last us until the next pickling season. I was praised and given money on New Year's Day for bowing with my head low to the ground. There was a long bus ride to school. I had a few cousins my age there, but we had never kept in touch. Several times a year photographs of strangers taken at amusement parks, graduations, weddings or at the family gravesite arrived in manila envelopes. Their clothes were like the ones people wore in the United States, but they didn't quite match in color or pattern. The secondary school-age cousins had identical haircuts and uniforms.

"You could get your ears pierced in Korea," added Mom as further incentive. All school year I had pleaded to no avail. "Maybe contact lenses. You always wanted them and in Korea, they're inexpensive."

I firmly believed that pierced ears and contact lenses were the only material possessions standing in the way of my ascension into the apex of junior high popularity. My chief ambition in life was to be popular, to fit in with the crowd of people who often went in groups driven by an older brother or sister to football games, pizza parlors, and private parties. With my mother's promise and my *TEEN* magazine makeover, I decided to go.

I met Faith several weeks after arriving. Prompted by my restlessness and my budding friendship with her young helper, Soon Dok, only two years my senior, my Aunty Heh-Dong hastened to find me another social outlet. Soon Dok was a servant and therefore, in my aunt's estimation, an entirely inappropriate companion. I had taught Soon Dok how to cartwheel across the living room floor and had begun to teach her English when my aunt found the notebook of words written in Soon Dok's awkward scrawl. The next morning my aunt announced: "I found you an American friend. She lives near us." She then announced Soon Dok was to be sent to work with another aunt.

That afternoon Faith stopped by the apartment and thereafter, much to the relief of my aunt, we were soon inseparable. We spent our days running around the building complex, pushing elevator buttons, climbing the railings, dropping balloons from the side of the building, and singing out loud to movie soundtracks. Spirited and mischievous, Faith was far more adventurous than my female cousins, deep into their exam preparations and who, when they weren't studying, played quiet indoor games and watched TV. And unlike Soon Dok, who was already burdened with the task of earning a living, Faith, like me, had few responsibilities.

She and her siblings Adam, Hope and Charity, lived six buildings down from where I was staying with Aunty Heh-Dong. My aunt, a former concert pianist, had suffered financial difficulty due to what the rest of the aunts hinted was some unscrupulous business practices of her husband, and as a result had been obliged to sell Grandpa's gift to her—a large traditional home with sloping black roofs, chamber pots, and a sizable inner courtyard in the middle of Seoul. By the time I arrived in Seoul, Aunty lived in a small flat in a complex of big, tall, indistinguishable blocks of concrete that dwarfed its residents. A few yellowing shrubs and heat-withered trees passed for landscaping, and the interiors revealed dusty granite stairs and small elevators. Dingy hallways and tiny balconies that displayed laundry drying on stands and plastic buckets of water, food or soaking clothes. The sidewalks of dull aching white blinded everyone in Seoul's noonday sun, and the parking lots held a handful of brilliantly polished black cars, identical except for their license plates. The smell of garlic, sweat, urine and sweet preserves clogged the air as the heat climbed, and the stickiness and scent relentlessly tunneled its way into my pores.

Whenever the opportunity arose, I basked in air conditioning. Air conditioning was the reason the relatives initially thought that I should live at my grandparents, but the days with my grandfather and step-grandmother were isolating. It was clear that calligraphy, shopping, and watching television alone led to childhood misery, so the relatives decided that I would stay at my English-speaking aunt's where I would have the companionship of numerous cousins. The cousins were initially intrigued by my arrival, but my inability to fully communicate in Korean and my presence was troublesome; another body only added to a cramped lifestyle. I didn't care. All I noticed was that the refrigerator held a container of black market Florida orange juice and huge blocks of my favorite food: neon orange American cheese.

On weekends my grandfather's chauffeured shiny black car picked me up, and I accompanied my step-grandmother on her errands and read alone. Dinners were quiet affairs served by my grandparents' helper on low black lacquer and mother-of-pearl inlaid tables under which I tucked my feet. I sat on the floor on flat silk pillows across from my grandfather, and enthusiastically practiced the old-fashioned Korean dinner etiquette that I knew would horrify my American mother: following my grandfather's lead, I chewed with my mouth open, slurped soup from my bowl which I held with two hands, and smacked loudly to show my enthusiasm for a delicious meal. I enjoyed picking and choosing my food with the click of my chopsticks: who needed serving spoons?

Yet air conditioning aside, I preferred the noise and bustle of Aunty Heh-Dong's where I planted myself in front of the gray metal fan and argued and chatted with my cousins in Konglish—a mixture of broken Korean and English.

The older relatives laughed at my rambunctious behavior, attributing it to my undisciplined American childhood, but the spoiled bratty boys were terrified—especially Aunty's favorite—her only son Doo Pyo, the household's pudgy nine-year-old crown prince. When Aunty wasn't around I would attack him with pillows and squirt water at his face, mimic his whining, and hide his favorite toys until he yelled, at which point I shrugged my shoulders and slyly said, "I was only having fun. Doo Pyo is a big baby." Doo Pyo endured my humiliation rather than fight back, and would fume and sulk as I sauntered off with a smirk. The teasing usually began after a lecture from Aunty on the importance of boys over girls, but much to Doo Pyo's relief, even the thrill of bullying ceased to hold my attention once Faith entered my life.

On our way back from one of the countless trips we made to Itaewon, Faith and I stopped by the shopping center near the apartment complex. Faith had been discussing what would make or not make a proper good-bye gift. Inside was a grocery selling huge vats of bean curd, large heads of cabbage, jars of peppers and spices, and packages of dried fish—eyeballs intact, like eclipsed moons staring into the sky. An old man squatting in front of the freezer fed a piece of honey-coated crispy candy to a little pink slippered boy as we cruised past. We veered towards a stall of women's clothing where designer brand knockoffs carpeted the wall as the smell of dried plums tickled my nose and the door jangled open.

On a dirty glass counter stood a rack holding key chains and a single imitation jade necklace, a teardrop of pale green plastic. Flecks of rusty brown were visible in the links of fake gold. I took a closer look; the plastic was chipped on the back. "Don't get me anything like that for a present. It's ugly," said Faith.

"Yeah," I said looking at it closely. We both knew a mere quarter could buy a real piece of jade. Faith was right; it was ugly.

Faith lived in a rigid world of absolutes, never wavering in her opinions about jewelry, boys or God. Having an opinion contrary to Faith's was never worth the inevitable debate it invited. She once pointed to a lunch box that featured the words 'Adam and Eve' in gold lettering.

"Adam and Eve were the first people on earth. Eve came from Adam's rib," said Faith.

"The cavemen—that's what we learned in social studies class."

"That's not what God says," affirmed Faith.

"You can't tell me you believe that every single person on earth came from these two people named Adam and Eve?"

"It's in the Bible," said Faith stubbornly.

"The cavemen are in every book you read about human evolution! You know, watchacallit. Cro-Magnon."

"What books?"

"Lots of books." I rolled my eyes.

"Aren't you a Christian?"

"Yeah. What does that have to do with evolution? Forget it," I said tactfully trying to avoid a religious discussion.

Every afternoon before the sun went down, my Aunty Heh-Dong took a walk around the apartment complex, carefully shielding her pale complexion with a large frilly beige umbrella. On one outing, conversation turned to religion and my aunt casually revealed she had converted to Catholicism years ago after studying in France. She said my grandfather, grandmother and great-uncle were Confucian, and that my uncles and aunts were Buddhists. There were also Protestants, including my Presbyterian father (except around Grandpa when Dad reverted back to Confucianism) and under her breath she scoffed that we even had a ridiculous relative who went to a shaman and an uncle who was briefly a communist.

"Why aren't we all one religion?" I asked Aunty Heh-Dong.

"We are all Korean. But I am Catholic. Your grandfather did not like that. Yes, I believe in God," she said importantly.

"Shouldn't we all be one religion since we're all in the same family?"

"Why? It's all the same."

After my conversation with Aunty Heh-Dong, I asked my older cousins about their religious preferences. They had laughed when I asked if they believed in God. They were university students, non-Christian Koreans—strong religious belief was fine for some, they admitted, but rather unimportant in their own lives.

I didn't tell Faith; I didn't want to hear what she would say. Who had ever heard of such a family? I imagined telling people back home about this and could see their incredulous faces, hear their hoots and disparaging remarks.

Pine Cove had taught me that silence was often easier. In the way she passed judgment, Faith shared some qualities of people back home, and so around her I did what I had learned to do to save myself from disappointment: guard my behavior, appear as if I knew exactly what I was doing at all times, and politely withhold my opinions whenever I disagreed. I went so far as to try to convince myself that whatever she said might possibly be right, especially when it came to subjects I wasn't certain of, in particular, God and Elvis Presley.

I listened to Faith ramble on about God with curiosity and skepticism. As I had neither the vocabulary nor the confidence to articulate my conflicting feelings about her God and remained undecided about my own, I never responded to her emphatic declarations. Elvis' existence and relevance was easier to grasp and debate.

When we passed the counter of knickknacks and hit a glass case filled with celebrity photos wrapped in plastic, I gazed at the familiar images with delight. The Osmonds. The Jacksons. Steve McQueen. Elvis Presley. American celebrities. She pointed to a picture of Elvis taken from the movie *Jailhouse Rock*. Slicked black hair, a lean body, and a mouth curled like a snail.

"Elvis is so cute," sighed Faith.

"Elvis?" I stared at a photo of a fat white-suited Elvis wearing huge sunglasses. "Him?" He looked like the man who sold my father the Ford Torino at the used car lot.

"Who do you like?"

"Lots of people. But not old Elvis. I don't like his long sideburns," I said.

"But he's handsome."

"When he was young. But not anymore," I declared. Faith detailed the reasons she liked Elvis and said that anyone who didn't like Elvis was probably immature. I ignored her, bought a wallet-size picture of the Jackson 5, and started rummaging around a stack of boxed sets of anklets.

Faith spoke Korean, ate Korean food, and lived in Seoul, but the U.S. was what we had in common, and it was the U.S. that Faith talked about, dreamt of, and wished for. Korea was temporary and the place we happened to be. For Faith, the daughter of a missionary, Korea was a home that she could never completely acknowledge—to do so would mean that she would have to ask when she would leave—and it was clear it wouldn't be for a very long time. Despite my background, it was always Faith who emphasized Korea's merits over the U.S. Pine Cove had taught me that it was best to try to do what everyone else did, and this meant labeling anything that wasn't American weird, unattractive, undesirable or ugly. I might have claimed Korean parentage, but I certainly wasn't going to say anything Korean was superior to anything American. I was an American, right down to the socks I wore on my feet.

"Socks are cuter in Korea. They have nice anklets here with lace. Or plain," said Faith. She held up a pair of blue and white anklets.

"You can get tons of socks in the U.S."

"Not like in Korea. Not like in Seoul. Plus, here you can buy them in boxed sets."

"I don't like Korean socks."

"Why not?"

"I just don't. They're weird." I couldn't think of a reason not to like the socks that I found myself tempted to buy, but I didn't want to agree with Faith. I also couldn't decide—would Korean socks pass muster in Pine Cove?

"When I'm in the U.S., I notice people don't have good socks," countered Faith. "Some things are better in Korea than in the U.S. They have nice clothes here. Better popsicles. And jewelry."

"I guess so." I imagined myself delivering Faith's spiel about Korean socks—I'd have the entire cafeteria laughing at me—instant social suicide.

"Isn't this cute?" she asked holding up a pink blouse.

"I like these," I said pointing to a blue sweater twin set. "I don't wear pink. Too girly." We headed back out by the jade necklace, still on the rack. It was untouched, but who would buy it? It had probably been there for months.

"Don't get me a shirt. I like those necklaces and earrings we saw in that Itaewon store. Not this one," she said flicking the teardrop imitation jade necklace with her fingers. "You don't have to buy an expensive present. Those gold and topaz earrings we saw weren't that expensive. Since I have red hair, brown really flatters me. *TEEN* magazine says earth tones are for redheads. I don't even need the matching necklace."

"Wanna get an *icha*?" I asked, tiring of Faith's jewelry talk.

"Sure. I'll treat. I got some money today," said Faith.

The sweet sunset pink freezer pops were jet-packed long and narrow and neatly tapered to a point. *Ichaba* my cousins said, resembled a mother's breast, but Faith and I thought that they looked like rockets. A small razor attached to a piece of string was tied to the freezer case and patrons would buy their *icha*, tear off the thin plastic covering, take the blade to the thick plastic and slice off the nipple. When I first started eating *icha*, I threw away the top, but noticing Faith slurp up the end, decided that my mother's worrisome airport gate lecture on the perils of Korean germs didn't necessarily include *ichas*. Faith was in excellent health and she ate an *icha* every day. Plastic ends were strewn all over the floor and a filmy coat of sticky juice on top of the freezer hosted a few daring flies. Faith and I would cut off the tips and voraciously suck out the fruity cold sweetness. I could never bring myself to litter, but Faith cheerfully threw her wrapper on the ground.

As we exited the shop, Faith licked the pink juice on her chin and asked, "What do you want from me as a going-away gift?"

"I don't know. Don't ask me. I haven't thought about it." I knew from Faith's specific hints that I would be obliged to buy her whatever she wanted or risk her disappointment, or worse, her disapproval.

Dangling amethyst earrings in ten karat gold plate, small chunks of light green jade on a bright red cord, thin silver bands that featured flowers or diamond cut topaz, and metal combs decorated with stones of tiger's-eye with tiny dragons etched on its sides—such Itaewon trinkets purchased with the money my relatives had dutifully presented to me in long white envelopes were now squirreled away in the corner pocket of my suitcase. Every so often I would dive into my inventory of presents and treasures and imagine myself at school, bedecked in new jewels, and presenting objects to friends.

At least once a week Faith and I took the bus to Itaewon where she baffled and bewildered storekeepers who were as impressed with her fluency as they were disparaging of my linguistic limitations. She had learned the art of bartering from Miss Hong and during negotiations would expertly cajole, plead, and stomp her feet. Feigning disinterest, she wouldn't hesitate to dismissively walk away from the seller. Itaewon merchants spoke English to cater to their clientele of GIs, young short-haired clean-shaven men who wandered the drag bargain hunting and admiring the logo T-shirts, sneakers and stereo equipment bound for export. With Faith, the shopkeepers spoke brusque Korean in stentorian voices and found themselves in an inevitable tug-of-war fighting hard for their end of the deal, exasperated and impressed by her ebullience and bargain savvy.

We ate hamburgers at Burger Palace or burritos at Tacoland and gossiped about boys—or mostly Faith did, specifically the two minister's sons Faith knew. They had ignored me the one time I had met them at her house. Faith would declare with authority that Mexican food at Tacoland tasted like Mexican food in Georgia. She hadn't been to the U.S. in four years, but I didn't say anything. Tacoland's decor of sombreros and guitars on the wall was similar to Mexican Villa back home, but Tacoland's beef burrito often gave me a stomachache.

"I think it tastes different," I said.

"Maybe. But just as good. Just as American," said Faith.

"Did you eat burritos a lot in Georgia?"

"Yeah, they have tons in Georgia." Tacoland's burritos were probably the only ones that Faith had ever eaten, but I knew better than to probe the matter. Faith would deny it and go so far as to intricately describe the burritos she never ate with her family after Sunday services, and might even throw in a subplot about a yellow velvet sombrero she had stored in her grandmother's attic.

The first time we went to lunch in Itaewon we each paid our own check. The second time Faith said we should take turns buying lunch, so I bought our meal. The third time Faith said she didn't remember I bought lunch the time before, so I paid again, and avoided asking myself if Faith was the kind of person who would deliberately forget her lunch money. Summer concluded with me having footed the majority of the lunches, but I felt obliged to share since I knew Faith didn't receive envelopes of money from relatives. One day as she watched me pull bills from my purse she explained her financial situation: "I get allowance, but Dad says we have to put most of it in the collection plate. God likes generosity," said Faith. That day in Itaewon, I bought the *ichas* and a bag of candy for us to share.

Faith's parents were strict. Her father yelled at Faith and several times he grounded her when I was at their apartment. When she was younger, he had whipped her with his belt. Faith was not allowed to go to dances (not that she was invited to any since she was homeschooled), couldn't watch movies with a PG rating, prayed before every meal, and had to wear skirts or dresses.

One day when I was sprawled on her sofa and thumbing through her copy of *A Pilgrim's Progress*, one of the few books her parents approved of, she commented on my clothing.

"You hardly ever wear a skirt or a dress," said Faith.

"So—"

"I wear culottes, like this," she said flashing me the shorts underneath the flap of her skirt. "We had them made here. My mom asked how come you never wear them."

"Since when do girls have to wear skirts?"

"I like skirts," said Faith defensively.

"I like shorts better. Don't you like shorts?"

"I can't wear them," said Faith. I tried to remember what I had read about Christian missionaries in my mother's *Ladies' Home Journal*. Faith admitted her church said no dancing. No shorts. No coffee. No Cokes. To play it safe, on my next visit I donned the mint green tent dress I had sewn in seventh-grade home economics class, the only one I had packed, a concession to my mother's insistence that I pack one dress. I was proud that I had sewn it without anyone's help. My mother had not bought it, it was not a hand-me-down from a cousin. That dress was a statement of independence.

"That looks very nice on you, Debbie," said Mrs. Cooke approvingly. Her mouse brown bouffant hairdo jiggled up and down and her lemon pursed mouth broke into a rare smile. Mrs. Cooke's skin was gray—smooth as a shark's fin. Though Seoul's heat was unbearable, I never saw her break a sweat.

"Thank you, ma'am," I answered politely. Mrs. Cooke beamed at my response. Having learned the word 'ma'am' from the Laura Ingalls Wilder books, I felt pleased to finally use it.

I found the Cookes bewildering, if not intimidating. If ever Reverend Cooke came home early, I went back to my aunt's, especially after the single time I had stayed to eat dinner.

It was a meal I would have longed for my mother to prepare. Slices of white bread in a green wicker basket. Frozen peas with a rim of yellow on their shells. Boiled carrots. Roast beef from the U.S. base that a parishioner had given Reverend Cooke. Mrs. Cooke brought out the white rice I had eaten nearly every night of my life, but it looked different when the Cookes were serving it from a Pyrex bowl with light blue cornflowers on the side. In the refrigerator was dessert—green Jell-O with canned fruit cocktail. I felt authentic. American.

Unlike Aunty Heh-Dong, the Cookes never bought black market products—coveted goods from the U.S. base that found their way on the shelves of local corner stores. Their Western food was from church members who lived on the base, or from care packages sent from home. All summer I had happily munched on pretzels and potato chips from Faith's pantry, and had envied the cans of Campbell soup neatly organized in alphabetical order. When I told Faith that my aunt ate American food purchased from the black market Faith had said, "Some people might call black market food a sin."

"A sin?"

"It's illegal and it's against the law. So it's like stealing. And stealing is one of the commandments."

After that conversation with Faith, I went back to my aunt's apartment, opened her refrigerator, looked at the orange juice, and found myself envisioning a jail term. I warned my aunt that she might get in trouble. I felt guilty for loudly expressing my desire for American food, pushing my family into what I now saw as serious criminal activity. "Illegal? It's cheaper this way. Besides, how else will I get this American food?" said Aunty Heh-Dong.

"From the U.S. base."

"Who do I know at the U.S. base?" she said. I began to monitor my orange juice drinking. I couldn't stop completely, but I sipped more slowly and tried not to fill my glass to the top. I didn't want to contribute to Aunty Heh-Dong's illegal sinful activity.

Pride enveloped my body as I sat down to dinner with Faith's family. I moved as if rehearsed, in sync with perfect notes, a divinely inspired meal, a choreographed moment, like the day the fly ball sweetly smacked my vinyl glove and I won the girls' softball league game without even trying. I was eating a meal that I had longed for and read about, gesturing the way television had showed me—holding hands for evening prayer, dabbing the corners of my mouth with a napkin, listening to the light chatter about church and God, and saying 'yes ma'am' and 'no ma'am.'

Synchronicity spun the room—a cuckoo clock went off at exactly six o'clock, calico patchwork pillows decorated the hard Quaker style chairs, and in the background wafted the lightest smell of lemon ammonia from the linoleum tile floor. Across from us sat Faith's little sister Charity with white blonde hair and a bright pink ribbon, a real life replica of the doll in the Pine Cove Mall toy store window. I felt certain that now was the time I would be magically transformed into the popular and scintillating eighth grade girl I yearned to be.

During dinner, Faith's sister Hope revealed that Miss Hong had lied about Charity's age to the ticket taker at the swimming pool—telling him Charity was three years-old, not four, in order to get cheaper admission. "Miss Hong was not telling the truth," said Hope solemnly. Reverend Cooke nodded like a slow lizard. I waited for his forked tongue to dart out and scoop up some peas. Mrs. Cooke's lips wrinkled like plastic wrap. Oblivious Faith continued to shove forkfuls of rice into her mouth, barely masticating her food, and I felt my heart grow weary for Miss Hong.

Next to Faith, Miss Hong was my favorite person in the Cooke household. Chatting and giggling, she darted about the house cooking and cleaning, scooping up Charity to kiss her, comforting Hope when she was crying, playfully joking with Adam and never losing her temper— even when she caught Faith and I sneaking around and playing with her makeup. I concentrated on eating a dark brown slice of roast beef with a blob of pink in the middle. I felt a knot in my throat; the roast beef was tough.

"Man. Oh, man," drawled Reverend Cooke, clearly disappointed in Miss Hong.

Faith's family said the word 'man' because to say 'God' was to take The-Lord's-Name-In-Vain. When I first heard Mrs. Cooke say 'man' I almost laughed out loud envisioning her in bell-bottom pants and love beads saying 'man' and 'far-out' and making a peace sign. After I heard Reverend Cooke, I realized that the Cookes weren't kidding about taking 'the Lord's name in vain.'

"Why would she do that? Man, a Korean will always lie to save a few pennies," said Reverend Cooke. He shook his head in disapproval. His black plastic Coke-bottle frames were ready to slide down his nose, a knob of bacon flesh, greasy and fat.

"Man," said Adam. "It's not that bad, though, is it Dad?"

"It's not right, son. Oh, man," repeated Revered Cooke. "That's a Korean for you. Oh, it's hard to tell the truth."

I felt like squirming but Faith had told me that her mother disapproved of fidgeting at the table, so I didn't budge. I took shallow breaths through my mouth; I was deep underwater avoiding the surface where a cloud of venomous bees swarmed overhead, to break it would be a wretched death by stinging. I was immovable and innocuous, a solid smooth stone at ocean's bottom.

"I tell you," he said with a nod of camaraderie, "You can't trust those Koreans when it comes to matters of money. They're a dishonest bunch. Don't you find that Debbie?"

Dishonest Koreans.

I shrugged. "Let's pray," he said taking me into his confidence.

We bowed our heads in silence and after Reverend Cooke said 'amen' the bread basket made its way around the table. Thank you, sir. Thank you, ma'am. Thank you, Adam, Faith, Hope and Charity. I coughed and Mrs. Cooke pointed to a glass of water. Peas that stuck to my throat. Roast beef that took two glasses of water to swallow. No spices. No garlic. No smell that lingered on your clothes. No fire on your tongue. No delicious fishy sweetness that made everything stink. It was the stink that made my friends back home hold their noses in jest when they came to my house, but that summer, I had finally come to realize it was redolent with memories of food and family.

I picked up a piece of bread as Mrs. Cooke's knee accidentally brushed mine under the table. Her thick support panty hose made a slick quiet buzz, like the sound of thousands of nylon zippers racing up and down. My mother had bought me my first pair of panty hose for the school chorus concert; I liked the way they clung to my legs, but after a few washings they lost their elasticity. I threw them away after someone at the bus stop told me that I had elephant ankles. Mrs. Cooke's panty hose were tight and snug against her leg.

Faith had once told me when we were doing makeovers at her house that she wore panty hose to church. "But my mom still won't let me wear makeup to church. I can wear it next year," Faith had said.

"I don't wear makeup. My mom says I don't need it. But she'd let me if I wanted to," I bragged. I hadn't ever asked. *TEEN* magazine never said what to do when you had eyes that looked like mine, and my attempts with makeup application left me with two eyes appearing to have been punched.

The Cookes' dinner finished early and I came home in time to eat peeled apples in front of the TV with Aunty Heh-Dong and my cousins. Usually I ate a few slices and then retreated into the back room to read while they watched a soap opera. This time I stayed, not wanting to be alone.

"Did you have fun with your little American friend?" asked Aunty Heh-Dong affectionately. "Debbie, my American niece."

My eyes began to water when I thought about dinner at the Cookes.' I concentrated on the old father on television with a bun on top of his head and a long beard brandishing his walking stick at his grown son with thick eyebrows. The sobbing mother wore a braided hairdo like reindeer antlers. In the middle of a shrill monologue she threw herself on the ground (amazingly not a single hair moved) and said she was going to kill herself if her disobedient ungrateful no-good son didn't listen to his elders.

Korea's elders were making me crazy. Reverend Cooke calling Koreans liars. Aunty Heh-Dong's lecturing on the superiority of boys over girls. Shopkeepers berating me for not speaking Korean. I felt my cheeks grow damp, pretended to rub my eyes and went into my room. Everyone was too engrossed in the program to notice. I opened my suitcase and looked at the presents I had bought for my family: two rings and a necklace for my mother, a necklace and haircomb for my sister, a back massager and an old-fashioned pillow for my father. Pine Cove was an ocean away.

Two days later, I was at Faith's getting ready to go back to my aunt's when Reverend Cooke came home early. On my way out the door

Reverend Cooke exchanged a glance with Faith and she said, "We didn't know you were Korean."

"What?"

"Yesterday your aunt told me at the store that your dad's Korean."

"Yeah," I said.

"We thought you said your dad was in the U.S. Army," said Faith sheepishly. "I mean, you know, American."

"He is. He's Korean, but a U.S. citizen."

"I see. Sure you won't stay for dinner, Debbie?" said Mrs. Cooke in her red-checked apron.

"Sorry, I can't. My aunt's expecting me." Meatloaf was on the table, slices of white bread were neatly fanned out in the green wicker basket, and there in the Pyrex bowl was one of my favorite foods: yellow canned corn. Miss Hong had baked brownies for dessert; Faith and I had snuck into the kitchen and devoured several pieces. The brownies were warm and buttery, melting as they touched my tongue.

Man, a Korean will always lie to save a few pennies.

"Is your Mom, American?" asked Reverend Cooke pleasantly. I knew what he was asking: so what are you really?

"My Mom is Korean, but from Hawaii," I said politely, to save their embarrassment, to save my own. Dad had told me saving face was Korean, yet here we all were, saving face and the Cookes were from Georgia.

"My Dad didn't know you were Korean," said Faith.

"I really thought you were all American," said Reverend Cooke with a pause.

I thought you were part-white.

"I'm Korean," I said. All summer I had longed to distinguish myself from the 'Korean-Koreans' as I called the locals, vehemently declaring my American birthright and culture, and resisting the idea of belonging to a group whose language and opinions I failed to understand. Now I claimed it. I'm Korean. The phrase bounced back; it buckled and shook and sturdied itself in a long winded tunnel of denial and echoes. The words hung on, balancing while my limbs became solid steel, and I didn't flinch but swung long and hard and heard the clean crack of defiance.

"Born in California, so I'm American, too." My toe curled and I scraped it against the carpet. I was sitting on the sofa and put my hand underneath my thigh and gave it a hard pinch. It felt good to have it hurt.

I had once told a woman at the Pine Cove mall I was a Vietnamese refugee, rescued from a boat after a march through the jungle, a helicopter ride and a parachute jump to flee the chaos of enemy fire. I spun stories about shimmying up coconut trees and fetching well water and getting excited when I saw my first toilet—mixing up the TV news reports on the Vietnam War with a few *National Geographic* specials on the South Pacific. The woman said, "Amazing, just amazing," but when Mom approached I excused myself, saying I had to help my Honorable Mother weave baskets —our family tradition, along with yak herding. I felt slightly guilty about the stranger's sincerity and my impersonation of refugees, but reasoned I might as well have some fun instead of reiterating the rather mundane story of my birth at Pine Cove hospital, and how except for one year in Seoul on the U.S. base during kindergarten, I had lived my entire life in this small town.

Faith and I were friends, but I was glad I was leaving Seoul. After she gave me my going away present, I wasn't sure what I felt about her.

I had made a special trip to Itaewon to buy her the pair of topaz and gold earrings. The saleswoman put them in a small velveteen box and I ran my finger against the fabric and opened and shut the box, the hinge neatly snapping back, the earrings and their tiny cuts sparkling clean and sharp. I held the topaz to the light and saw the sun push through the color. I closed my eyes and imagined the stone shattering. When I opened my eyes I started to count the tiny diamond shapes. I was tempted to keep the earrings for myself.

When Faith opened her gift she let out a small squeal: "I love these. They will look so good with my hair." Faith presented me with an oversized box wrapped in remnants of Santa Claus wrapping paper that carried bits of scotch tape from the last time it was used. Inside was the imitation plastic jade necklace in the shape of a teardrop with the chip on the back from the store down the street, the gold chain faded to a dull brown.

"Thanks," I said softly.

"I thought it would look good on you. Jade is really nice. I got it in Itaewon." Faith studied my confused and crestfallen face and quickly said, "I remembered you didn't have a necklace in that shape." She flicked her new earrings back and forth in her ear as I watched the gold hit the light. The reflection hurt my eyes. I knew Faith would never count the diagonal cuts or hold the stones up to the sky and imagine she was floating among the stars beyond the Milky Way. She hummed an Elvis

Presley tune and covered her lids with green eye shadow. "Do you want some makeup for the picture?"

"No."

She finished her makeup and we walked up to the roof of the apartment and took pictures with my camera. "Mail me a copy. Here, I'll pose against the ladder," she said draping her body against the rungs like a fashion model. "Promise you'll write once a week and send a copy of my picture."

After I said good-bye to Faith, Miss Hong gave me a hug and told me to come back and visit, and Charity gave me a kiss good-bye. On the way to my aunt's I gave the necklace to a little girl on the street. She took it without thanking me and ran away calling out to her friends down the alley.

I was driven to the airport in Grandpa's shiny black car and boarded the plane eager to go home. In my pierced ears were twenty-four karat gold earrings given to me by Aunty Heh-Dong, and in my backpack were my brand-new contact lenses. I stopped over in Hawaii and learned of Elvis Presley's death while eating freshly picked white sour sop from my great-Aunty Esther and great-uncle George's yard. I found myself humming *Love Me Tender* and great-Aunty Esther told me she always liked the movie *Blue Hawaii*. I wondered when Faith would hear the news about Elvis Presley.

A few weeks after school began, I wrote Faith a double-sided four-page letter. I wrote with a different ink color on every line, tearing up pages when I made a mistake, and copying it over several times. I thought about her rushing to read the letter to Miss Hong and her plans to see me the next time she visited the States. I thought of our trips to Itaewon and baking chocolate chip cookies, and asked if she had been to Tacoland recently. I confessed that Korea had changed my perspective on life, that I was lucky to have visited Seoul, and that I was glad to have met her. I told her about my friends, my crush in math class, and my plans for the school year.

I thought about Faith and I taking buses, running outside under the tall buildings and imitating the knife sharpener's call to the delight of Miss Hong. *Kahl gah say yo. Kahl gah say yo.* Pine Cove friends would never know the thrill and fear of running through an outdoor market dodging dried squid with long tentacles and huge plastic bags of orange teddy bears to escape the wrath of a spoon-waving old woman. They never felt the warm monsoon rain on their skin and would never understand how life could orbit around an old gray metal fan. They would say Miss Hong spoke funny English instead of admiring her elegant long eyes and wide fat laugh. Faith knew. Her bossiness didn't seem overbearing from so far away. I studied the photos I enclosed in the envelope. In the picture I took, she was frowning. The photo she took of me was equally disappointing, mouth agape, eyes closed, hair messy and uncombed. We had forgotten to take one of us together.

Our social studies course that year covered the early Spanish missionaries and the Indians. I pictured Reverend Cooke in a long burlap robe and woven sandals, carrying a big wooden cross and locking up the native girls in dark cells to pray, keeping them away from their families and telling them they were untrustworthy sinners and liars. Were sinners sinning if they didn't understand sin? It didn't make sense.

Faith was a friend to me, I thought, feeling both more and less certain as I looked at her picture. I made a scrapbook of my trip and when I didn't hear anything from Faith, I sent another letter a month later, worried that she didn't receive it. I checked the mailbox every day, patiently waiting for a reply. Yes, Faith had been my friend. I didn't have any doubt that we were, and I knew that she had been just as lonely as I had been before we had met. It was a good summer.

A year later, Faith wrote a short postcard. On the front was Elvis Presley strumming his guitar: 'Elvis is the best. I'm visiting Georgia in the fall. Write back. Love, Faith'. Everyone knew Elvis had died.

As for Faith going to Georgia, it was difficult for me to believe that she was going back home to live. I realized she felt I had abandoned her, and that she wanted me to know that she too would eventually leave Korea. It was too much for Faith that the Korean American girl had the freedom of pocket money and an American life awaiting her at the end of the summer. And without understanding it, I saw Faith's friendship as validation, as she was everything that Pine Cove would accept, everything I thought I was supposed to be.

I took the scrapbook from Korea off of my bookshelf and noticed that I had two pages left at the end where I had intended to glue a few coins and bills. Instead, I carefully put Faith's postcard in on the next to the last page and wrote at the side: *My Friend Faith—Seoul, August, 1977.*

THE LADIES OF SHEUNG WAN

She couldn't take another step.

Maybe I'll just stop for a moment, Yuk Ki said to herself. Just sit, right here. She didn't. She knew what would happen if she sat down on the steps of the neon-lit café in Sheung Wan; it wasn't a fancy place, but it was filled with people in clean clothes. More than that, if she sat, she was giving in. She looked down the street: Che Sum was nowhere in sight. She leaned against her handcart and tried to shut out the noise from the city.

Yuk Ki had bowlegs shaped like a bent iron magnet and a spine so curved it forced her to twist her neck like a turtle to see anything but the ground. Most of the time, Yuk Ki didn't care; she knew the way they looked at her pushing her handcart stacked with cardboard—this was just life. It wasn't her fault her son died. Yes, she had thrown her daughter out of the house, but at the time Moy was nothing but trouble; and besides, it had been ten years since Moy had left Hong Kong. She was in Canada. Children don't do what they should for their parents. Didn't matter. She got on fine by herself.

Years ago, she and Ming Ho sold newspapers; they even had their own stand by Wing On Department Store when business was really booming, but the stand went bust. The 7-Elevens really killed them. Who wanted to buy a newspaper from old people on a corner when you could get it at 7-Eleven? By the time Ming Ho died, they were back where they started, out on the street, sitting on the cement steps down from Cat's Alley with a stack of newspapers and an old basket of coins. Back then she and Ming Ho would talk to Che Sum whenever she passed them. The three would take a quick break and then Che Sum would be off, pushing her handcart down the street.

Collecting cardboard for recycling was hard work, but after Ming Ho died, Che Sum had helped her get a handcart and showed her what cardboard pieces were best, how to stack and tie everything properly so things wouldn't slip off. Lean and wiry, Yuk Ki was ten years Che Sum's senior, but she managed to push the load up Wellington from Queen's Road, right past that fancy new gym, slow to be sure, but she made it like everybody else.

Lately, the junction seemed steeper; it took longer to get around the curve. The slight slope was like a long steep hill and she found herself taking a break on the cement island in the middle of the road waiting for lights to change *red-green-red-green-red-green*, massaging the back of her neck with her stiff hands, before she finally shoved off to move the handcart. People never liked it when she stood there for too long; women shuddered and shrank away, fearful their skirts would brush her. When they looked, men said, get out of the way old woman.

—You get out of the way, she'd answer defiantly behind her cart. You'd smell like garbage too, if you spent your days picking from the dumps, she wanted to say, but never did. Drivers honked when she didn't cross the street fast enough, but they never hit, at least not her, not yet.

She and Che Sum were meeting up as they often did, to exchange news or eat rice. Now and then the two women worked together, but more often than not, they each spent their day alone. Yuk Ki waved when she saw Che Sum down the block and watched her navigate the cart through the narrow street between taxicabs.

—Lots of boxes. People moving in that new building, said Che Sum. We can go back after lunch. Hot today. Hey, sit down.

—I'll sit, said Yuk Ki. She didn't sit but stood looking at the crowd. Lunchtime. Everyone was hungry, rushing to eat, impatient to get back to work. She was hungry.

It was hot; the weather had turned and the chill had left the air. The wet heat clung to their bodies and hung in the air like layers of steam. The city was waiting for the monsoons, summer rains to wash away the grime—the spit on the sidewalks, the dust from construction, the stench of car fumes and garbage.

—Shoes look good, said Che Sum.

—Comfortable. High quality. These will last a long time, said Yuk Ki.

Yuk Ki was finally comfortable in the shoes Che Sum had retrieved from the dump by the new apartment complex on Queen's Road. Che

Sum had presented Yuk Ki the new footwear after watching her friend slip on a rainy day.

—Slippers are fine, but us old women need all the help we can get, Che Sum had told Yuk Ki. Take off your slippers. Here. These are almost new.

—These are kids' shoes.

—Just be glad they're not the kind with the flashing red light on the back. Those would be good though. Especially when it gets dark.

—Nothing wrong with my slippers.

—Old woman, don't be silly. Here wear the shoes. Don't tell me I spent all that time digging them out of the dump and you're not going to wear them!

When Yuk Ki's back had started hurting more, Che Sum had said that they should work as a team. They both knew that it would mean less money, though now and then when it came out the same, Che Sum casually said that it was more profitable to work together. Yuk Ki put up a protest so as not to appear needy and Che Sum said what was proper, that Yuk Ki was doing the favor, when it was really the other way around.

Yuk Ki hesitated before the stoop of the Sheung Wan café and then eased her bottom onto the step.

—Good idea, said Che Sum. Sit down. We need a short break. Too much work. Oh, the heat is bad today. Work slow. That's best. I'll get something to drink. What do you want?

—Water, said Yuk Ki.

—Wait right here, said Che Sum. She scuttled across the street and came back with a bottle of water.

—Here, said Che Sum. I told you, sit down. Sit down! Right here on the step. Che Sum pulled out a handkerchief from her pocket and dabbed Yuk Ki's forehead. Yuk Ki shifted her posture; she slumped her shoulders, closed her eyes, and patted Che Sum's hand.

—I'm fine. Just sitting for a minute. So hot today, said Yuk Ki. Sure, the manager might try to push them, maybe dump water on them, who knows, but it wouldn't be for awhile. They could afford to sit.

—Yes, let's take a rest, agreed Che Sum.

The cafe manager came out and started to yell.

—Get off old woman! Get off!

Che Sum growled right back, ready to scowl at anyone who dared to take a sidelong glance at Yuk Ki.

—Don't worry, Yuk Ki, just take a breath, said Che Sum patting her on the shoulder. Yuk Ki nodded, sweating in the noonday heat as her hand gripped the wall. You just sit—rest, said Che Sum, her gruff voice softened with worry.

The manager went back inside. Yuk Ki glanced at her friend's navy blue flowered shirt, black cotton pants, and fabric shoes, and looked down at her own equally dirty pair. Two old women, that's what we are, like shriveled pieces of dried ginger. Che Sum is younger, but still an old woman. The police were sure to tell them to move along. Bastards. No respect for elders.

There was the day a woman had shouted for them to get out of the dumpster, called them names. Usually Che Sum yelled back or ignored people, but young Che Sum didn't fight back. Old Yuk Ki had stepped in.

—Leave us alone! Stupid woman, said Yuk Ki. Squawk. Squawk. You sound like a chicken!

—Let's go, said Che Sum.

—That building's a waste of time. Don't listen to her, said Yuk Ki. Forget it. Let's go eat. Forget about that squawking woman.

Che Sum was quiet.

Everyone gets tired. Who would look after her friend, Che Sum? Silly really, she's the one who watches me, thought Yuk Ki.

—You sit, said Che Sum. That fool's always like that.

—Maybe five minutes, said Yuk Ki. She didn't want to sit. But it was hot.

Che Sum nodded. She touched Yuk Ki's spotted gnarled hands. Yuk Ki pressed her deep brown cheek against the cool of the mint green tile. People passed and someone spit near their feet. When the café door swung open and patrons spilled out, the welcome draft of chilly air quickly disappeared.

—So hot, said Yuk Ki, letting the heat push her down. It didn't seem so bad to give in a little. What would she have ever done without Che Sum? Even now, working together—Che Sum could do better on her own.

—You just sit, said Che Sum, fanning her friend. The rain's coming.

The warm rain began to fall, and the steps became slick with water. Yuk Ki looked at Che Sum's hot and sticky face and smiled. Che Sum—a good friend. Like a sister.

—How can I worry about five years from now if I can't figure out five hours from now, Che Sum had always told Yuk Ki.

—You're young, Yuk Ki had said, emphasizing her seniority. You need to think about the future. At my age, it's different. Che Sum had brushed the comment aside; younger people didn't listen.

Yuk Ki slowly sipped water from the bottle.

—Stay right there, Che Sum said, looking at her friend. You need to rest. I'll cover the cardboard. Che Sum got up and began covering the stacked cardboard with strips of black and clear plastic, garbage and grocery bags cut in half, and woven vinyl tarps of blue and red stripes.

Yuk Ki agreed. A little rest might be good. Doesn't mean anything. Just five minutes. The café customers were carefully stepping around them but Yuk Ki's eyes were closed. All she could hear were the jackhammer voices collapsing into the sounds of the street.

—She's getting sick right here. You need to do something about this scum, ruining my business, the manager yelled to the policeman across the street. The policeman ignored him until a few people began to block the narrow sidewalk.

—The old woman's dying. Get an ambulance.

—What's happening?

—Get those carts out of the road, old woman.

—Drive around them, Che Sum barked to the driver. You rest, she told Yuk Ki.

—Yes, whispered Yuk Ki. She felt her heart rapidly beating. She wanted to reassure her friend. Young Che Sum shouldn't worry; she looked so small and frail. Yuk Ki wanted to speak, but settled for squeezing Che Sum's hand.

Che Sum huddled next to her, silently weeping as she fanned Yuk Ki with a shred of torn cardboard. As the slight wind of the fan hit her forehead Yuk Ki thought of the day on the ferry, tiny Moy wrapped in a blanket. The wind skipped off the harbor and Moy wriggled and smiled.

—It's going to be fine. Yuk Ki, Yuk Ki! Don't worry, don't worry. I'll take care of the cart, Che Sum cried.

People were shouting and strangers had gathered. The policeman stood nearby but Che Sum rocked Yuk Ki in her arms, holding her close and sobbing. A soft wind carried a few plastic bags away and the cardboard became wet, large drops of water coming down on the brown flattened boxes.

—Summer rain, that's all, Che Sum said to Yuk Ki. It's no problem, Yuk Ki. You can rest now. Just take your time.

Yes, Yuk Ki wanted to say. Don't worry Che Sum. The slip into sleep is nothing. The relief of a warm bath. A cool drink on a hot day. The colors run blue and black behind closed eyes. Very pretty and all so fast. The waiting is bad—but now it's close, so close. Nothing to fear, just a rest, she wanted to say. But she was too tired to speak.

SWIMMING IN HONG KONG

FROGGY

She swam halfway, but this time, instead of turning around and paddling where she entered, she came straightforward and with a little help from the rope, got out at the opposite end of the pool—the finish line. She didn't seem as discouraged as she did the week before. I gave a wave as I always do, and she smiled back. These things take time but I knew it was a good sign. She's going to eventually swim a lap, that's what I told Fei Yun and Arnie. Arnie didn't believe me. Then again, Arnie's always been like that, ever since primary school. I've known him for fifty years and if he hasn't changed yet, he's not going to.

"She hasn't made it yet and she's been coming here for six months," said Arnie.

"She's made it halfway," I pointed out.

"I don't think she can do it. What do you want to bet?"

Arnie's always betting. A couple of times about ten years ago, he won money at the races. That made him feel like a big-time gambler until his wife Cherry told him that he had a choice between gambling and spending money on his grandson. That stopped it, though she lets him buy Mark Six tickets if the pot's really big. Every now and then, he likes to act as if he can still bet.

"No bet," I said.

"Why not, if you are so sure?"

"No betting. I just know. Her stroke is better. I notice her breathing has improved."

"Froggy knows. I think she's going to make it. Whether that's in my lifetime or not is the real question," chuckled Fei Yun.

I have had the nickname Froggy for as long as I can remember. I learned to swim growing up in the New Territories and when we moved to Kowloon during my high school days, I even won a few swimming prizes. Arnie remembers. Swimming is not the only reason they call me Froggy. I'm bowlegged, too.

Two times a week, Fei Yun, Arnie and I come to the Victoria Park pool with a bunch of other old man regulars. We were coming before we all retired and we'll be coming up until our last days. Lately, I come almost every day.

About six months ago this woman started coming to the pool. She's black. I overheard her telling the pool attendant that she was American. To be honest, it is the first time I've seen a black woman up close in a swimming suit. I've seen them wearing what looks like a swimming suit on those singing television programs my grandchildren watch. But not in a real one. Come to think of it, I don't think I've seen a black woman swimming at the Olympics. She's slender, lean muscle and not so big. The pool attendant told me later that she's trying to train as a triathlete: biking, swimming and running.

She's not a very good swimmer. The first time I saw her splashing around the pool she was gasping and flailing her limbs about. I thought she was in a panic, the worst thing you can do in the water. Then I realized she was grabbing onto the dividing rope and she was kicking, but nothing was wrong with her. I couldn't save her anyway if she was drowning. Not at my age. She would drown me! That's why we have the lifeguard! That's why we pay the fees! Anyway, she was hard not to notice. Gradually, her paddling began to take the shape of a crawl and she would go about ten feet before turning around and starting again. Her eyes would widen right before she went underneath the water, and you could tell by the way she kept trying she was going to improve. She's much better than when she first started.

I have a lot of respect for people who learn to swim as adults. My wife, Suk Mei, couldn't swim if her life depended on it. I tried to teach her when we were first married, but I wasn't patient as a young man and after a couple of lessons where I ended up yelling at her, she didn't try again. I can't say I blame her. I taught my daughter and sons how to swim but all of those years we spent together, my wife would watch me swim from the beach or a poolside bench. She said it didn't matter to her whether or not she could swim, but it would have been nice for her to learn. Sometimes when I am swimming in this pool I half expect her to be there when I surface. She died three years ago.

My youngest son Man Ho and I didn't speak for years before Suk Mei died. It was after I sent him to school in the UK and he had come back and was making a lot of money. A big shot. He came back thinking he was better than everyone including his own father. Bad son.

He had said to me, "If I listened to you, I never would have made anything out of my life. What do you know?"

"I know enough to break my back to work for you and give you everything," I had yelled at him. "Get out of my sight. Go back to England."

Suk Mei cried. He had that fancy education, but it didn't teach him anything. Who speaks like that to his own father? No respect. I'm the father. I knew better. He didn't understand. He still doesn't sometimes. I forgave him before Suk Mei died. Man Ho wasn't like my other kids, he always pushed the hardest and in my heart I know that's why I loved him the most. I still do, even if I can't stand looking at how fat he's become. His body looks like a dumpling. Me, too, but I'm an old man.

I don't think the American is married. You don't get many black people in Hong Kong except around the mosques or in Central, but I'm never in Central and the only reason I was around the mosque in Tsim Sha Tsui before was because my acupuncturist used to have an office there. Anyway this is different, and she is always alone.

The day she swam halfway across I passed her right before she hopped into the pool. She nodded her head and smiled and I walked over to talk to Fei Yun. She seemed quiet, not that I've ever heard her speak, but her shoulders were a little slumped, as if she were sad or tired. Usually she smiles a good deal but this time her mouth was in a straight line. Solemn. Troubled. That's why it's good to swim. I may have worries but after I get into the pool they peel away from my body. The cool water rushes over you, a wonderful silence coats and bathes, washes everything away. In water, I feel younger than I do on land, memory flooding muscles and bones, aches disappearing. Yes, she looked like she needed to swim that day. Life is like that. There are days we all want to swim away, though the older I get, the less I have that feeling. I want to stay around as long as I can. No need to swim far, just back and forth in the pool is enough. I was glad when she walked forward to the end of the pool instead of turning around. I could tell she felt better.

RUTH

It's a start and one must start someplace. I made it halfway and then paddled and walked to the far end of the pool. Half a lap. It's getting me ready for the real thing. Usually I wade and paddle back, but not this time. Call me anything, but I'm not a quitter.

The old man in the brown swimming trunks, the one with the long eyes and sad smile gave me a little nod. He's here whenever I am, swimming lap after lap, steady and smooth, absolutely mesmerizing, the way he cuts through the water. He never seems to tire and when he swims he's all grace and agility, as if it's the most natural thing in the world for him to be submerged in the water. He does the breast stroke, hits the surface like an otter, his head bobs up for a second, catches some air and then he's down again. When he climbs out I'm always surprised, he really is an old man, but in the water, you wouldn't know it.

I laugh when I think of what I must have looked like to people when I first started, or even now: a black woman desperately trying to swim to the other side, splashing all over the place, week after week, wading back as she can't get across. After years in Asia, I'm used to curious looks. Some are friendly, greeting, nodding and watching, others never get rid of their prejudice. In Hong Kong I learned that you have to dive in because no one will wait around and ask you nicely if you're ready. Once you're in, it's a different story. You meet who you need to meet, but this is not a place for the timid.

I almost drowned when I was nine. As a child, my mother's ambition conspired with affluent day schools looking to diversify. I was good at school. My peers had homes with bathrooms larger than our apartment. One weekend I was invited with a few other girls to a friend's cottage near a lake. I wanted to fit in and couldn't admit I could barely swim. The next day we were supposed to all jump off the pier and go out on a boat. To prepare, I secretly snuck down by the lake to try to practice when I thought everyone else was playing near the house. Luckily my friend's older sister pulled me out of the water. I cried with relief and shame. She tried to show me how to float, but I refused. The next day she kindly took me to town for ice cream when everyone went out on the boat. I spent the weekend playing near the cottage and reading. The older sister must have said something because I was never invited there again. I didn't tell my parents. For years I avoided the water. It meant fitting in. I'd try, in fits and starts. Slowly. Little by little. Lessons here and there. But I never found a need to swim until six months ago. I decided it was time. The triathlon—I wanted to do it.

It's taken a long time for me to get this far swimming—six months to hit the middle, but I'll make it across. I learned that from running, the challenge of pushing through, it's that easy and that hard. I've never been a good swimmer but as masochistic as it sounds, I'm a great believer in doing whatever it is you find difficult. This is both positive, when it comes to work, and dare I say negative when it comes to relationships: some are difficult for a reason—and there is no need to hang around!

Some days when all I want to do is to jump in the water and swim all the way to India, from work and everything else in my life, I say to myself I'm good at leaving, though I'm not sure if it's true anymore. I find myself growing older and less comfortable with picking up and moving which is disturbing, because I am not certain where it is that I want to be, but I don't think it's here. People back home ask why I'm still in Hong Kong. It's a perfectly valid question and one I periodically return to myself but I've been an expatriate for many years and have lived in many places—London, Sydney, Rome, Tokyo. I have no plans to go Stateside and remain unconvinced about the benefits of American life. Or maybe it's that there's nothing for me to return to, no one to return for.

Earlier that day before swimming, my boss, the definition of the glory seeking, Ivy League educated elitist, refused to give me lunar New Year's *laisee*—having an Ivy League education myself, I feel perfectly entitled to call him that. If I had been in any other office in Hong Kong, I would have received a slim New Year's red envelope with crisp bills from the bank, as not only have I been an employee at this architecture firm for four years, but I'm single. He's Chinese, but spent twelve years in the U.S. and while illustrious institutions do not necessarily breed a reprehensible lot he, unfortunately, has failed to distinguish himself from the pack. He's the typical self-aggrandizing East Coast educated type of man seemingly hell-bent on making other's lives miserable. Tyrants of his ilk have a remarkable geographic mobility—they're everywhere. It's actually astounding how people like him feel the need to spread their horrid personalities across the continents.

Our office is white, glass and steel. Neat employee lockers in perfect slate gray. Small cubicles of clear soundproof boxes, an office of the present, future and past. I confess to admiring the sleek lines and precision, the fact that everything is perfectly accounted for, measured and thought out—down to the height of an unsharpened pencil, so that when you place the pencil in your exquisite company issued pencil holder, the shelf space will barely skim its pink eraser. The office lighting in meeting rooms magically erases fine lines and succeeds in making your skin appear smooth and supple. Everything is designed to make employees productive and put clients at ease. The talent it took to create this and other structures is inarguably stupendous. Yet talent, I have long realized, doesn't have anything to do with being a tolerable human being, which he, my boss, the creator of this space, is most certainly not.

He stood by the door to my office and then in a loud booming voice that everyone in their cubicles could hear said, "You're too old for *laisee*. It's for single people who aren't married. You're so old, you're supposed to be giving *laisee* away and already married."

Too old. He knows I'm forty-one. Janice, one of my colleagues heard and so did Charlie. They thought it was nasty, if not cruel of him to say that. I'm the only Westerner in the office, so he probably thought he could get away with it.

"Too old. It's not about that. You're supposed to say, 'Happy New Year Ruth, wishing you all the best and I hope you get yourself a good husband this year and have much happiness.' Age has nothing to do with New Year's etiquette," I said and watched him slink away towards the water cooler.

He didn't respond. Like all Ivy Leaguers, he shudders to think he's behaved in a gauche manner. The nature of his personality is such that to ignore him invites further insults. He's a few years older than I am and always comments on my hair, my clothes, something personal. It's never a compliment, more of an observation, as in 'you changed your hair,' or 'you're wearing red, you never wear red' or 'you lost weight'. Or he'll insult me and publicly state that my Cantonese is lousy after living here for ten years. Or bring up my marital status. (He doesn't know about my divorce, but that's my business.) It's subtle, but Janice notices.

"He likes you. You know. *Likes* you. I think he finds you attractive," she said delicately.

"Oh, for god's sake. Please do not even say those words."

"Why?" she giggled.

"Why? He's married with three children and he is absolutely the last person I would want to imagine in that kind of scenario."

"That's true. He's not someone anyone would like. But he likes you. That's why he's so mean."

"He likes me so much that he cuts my salary twenty percent, makes me work on Sundays and calls me at all hours of the night and day to tell me to come into the office. He even says I'm too old to get married. Last week he said he thought I looked as though I'd gained weight. All I can say is if that's his idea of affection, I pity the woman he loves. The man is a true beast."

"No," she paused. "You know when children are on the playground and one child likes another, maybe he hits her to show affection? It's like that. Very immature."

"That's right. Nursery behavior. That's ridiculous. I'm not interested. Why would I find him the least bit interesting?"

"Because he's rich and is your boss?"

"He's married, drives his employees into the ground, and let's face it, he hasn't hit the gym in the last ten years. On a personal level, I'm single, but I'm not desperate. There may not be a lot of jobs out there, but there are definitely other men."

I sounded funny, but I was fuming. Janice laughed. Charlie heard the last part and raised his eyebrows.

I didn't add, but it was clearly understood, that there would never be a romance between us! I am loathe to ponder that twisted brain of his which is probably filled with adolescent jungle bunny *National Geographic* fetishes I don't want to explore. The combination doesn't happen much anyway. It does in Jamaica; my father's sister married a Chinese man, but it's a rare occurrence outside of that world.

Make that overall in Hong Kong. Dating isn't easy here. It's not as if I'm looking only to date a black man, and I never dated much anyway. I had a brief marriage to a white British journalist by way of Eton and Oxford whose family thought me exotic. I believe that my Josephine Baker hairdo (then) and Italian language skills might have fueled the perception. My family just wanted him out, they were incredibly racist, but there were other reasons the marriage failed. Make that specifically *a* reason. She's got him now.

I focus on my work. I run. I'm learning to swim. When we buried my father in Jamaica, I looked out onto the blue and imagined him swimming there years ago, stopping at the well to get water on the way back home to the weathered wooden shack. That old dusty road, the sections of grass and black rocks and sand. The tree he described as being so tall, the tallest tree he'd ever seen, and the ripe guava you'd want to grab from the branch. He would tell us stories about his life, his language becoming lyrical as the stories unfolded, aching with longing for the village he left. He never went back after he came to the U.S.—so he left a beautiful land and blue water, desperate hot sun and sand that burned your eyes with its whiteness, for the American dream.

His home and what he left behind was hard to square with the adult I knew, the man who navigated cold gray sidewalks and tall buildings. Sometimes when I'm in the New Territories and look out at the sea, especially when I'd get to those places where there are so few people I could really be anywhere at anytime, I try to imagine him. Not as my father, but as someone I didn't know, a boy with everything before him, oceans away from his future. He always said he was a good swimmer, but the way he struggled and where we lived—there was never time for him to show me.

FROGGY

She stopped at the halfway point.

The last three times I've seen her, that's what has happened. She's hit a plateau.

Fei Yun shook his head, "Not in my lifetime."

"Be quiet," I said loudly.

Fei Yun shrugged his shoulders. "She's getting discouraged." You can always count on Fei Yun to be gloomy. He had some hard times as a kid in China; during the war his parents and sisters died. He always says, the war taught him to prepare for the worst. And later after nearly his whole family died, during those bad years, he swam to Hong Kong. Tolo Harbor. Takes guts.

"A piece of wood can save your life," is all he usually says about it, other than the cousin he left with drowned. Fei Yun's done well. He's got a business. Import-export. Don't ask him to talk about the old days in China, the Great Leap Forward. Telling everyone they had to make steel. Those were bad times.

"We had to take our pots and pans. Everything. Melt it all down. You know what you get when you throw a pot on the fire?"

"No," we all say. We do this every time.

"A pot that won't melt," he says. That's when he decided to leave. Just him and his cousin.

Arnie was the one who sounded hopeful. "I think she'll make it. She needs some technique advice."

"Her breathing is slowing her down. She comes up too soon for air. She needs to turn her head all the way to the side," I said.

"I think it's her kick," said Arnie.

"It's both," I said. "The crawl is very difficult. People are fooled. Took me a long time. Did you see her on TV?"

"For what?" asked Fei Yun. "Singing?"

"Now why would she be singing?" I said. "What makes you think she can sing?" Why would a famous singer be swimming three times a week in a public pool in Victoria Park! Sometimes Fei Yun is so thick. "No, she was running in the marathon."

"Didn't see it," said Fei Yun. "Marathon, eh?"

"Did she win?" asked Arnie. I knew he was thinking he should have placed a bet.

"No, she was running in it," I said. I lied. She was actually walking on TV, she looked tired. "She runs very fast."

"Then why can't she swim?" asked Arnie.

"What does swimming have to do with running, you stupid idiot!" At this point I had to walk away. After fifty years, talk like this can really get on your nerves.

When the black woman hoisted herself up out of the pool, I waved and told her to stop. At first when she happened to pass me she wouldn't say anything. I understand some English, but I'm not really comfortable saying much. She speaks some Cantonese. Good morning. Hello. Bye-bye. I showed her how the elbow pulls back in tandem with the head as it turns to the side like a clock, the teeth, the cogs moving in synchronicity. She tried it at the side of the pool while I watched. Then she said, thank you, got in, and prepared to do a lap.

All three of us stood by and watched. I told Arnie and Fei Yun they really should go away, not make such a big deal about it, but of course they just went about three steps and kept looking over their shoulders watching to see if she could do it, all the while pretending to towel off.

She almost got it. She made it about two-thirds of the way across. Fast learner. She didn't turn her head quite like she should, but her stroke was much better. She grinned and paddled to the end of the pool, using the divider ropes. She did it two more times, not going all the way, maybe half.

I thought to myself that there must not have been anyone to teach her. Maybe no one in her family knows how to swim. What do they think of her living so far away in Hong Kong? I remember when Man Ho was in England. I was always worrying, though never out loud because Suk Mei was always going on about it, so someone had to pretend that it was fine he was so far away.

What's she doing here so far away from her family? Her parents must be worrying. There could be a number of reasons why she didn't learn to swim as a child. Did anyone know she was swimming now?

My sons were fine swimmers, the youngest, Man Ho, could swim the butterfly. Perfect kicking, just like a dolphin. You'd never know it looking at him; he's such a fat bastard. Last week at the restaurant, I told him he ate too much.

"Slow down. Moderation," I said to him.

"I'm not eating much," he said defensively.

"You eat too much, you won't live long," I said. It's about the only thing I can tell him these days.

"I'm living well. Those who live well, live long," he said licking the tips of his chopsticks. For a moment when he looked at me, I saw him as a baby, nearly bald, with an open round face, chubby arms and fists waving in the air. I didn't say anything.

One vacation I put him in a tiny inner tube and pulled him around a pool, letting it glide along the water as the waves rippled out, skimming the surface. I used to skip stones. I could skip them maybe seven or eight times. My kids couldn't do that growing up in the city. We took them to the parks on the weekend, but it's not the same.

Funny the details you remember about growing up. Out in the New Territories I always had plenty of places to run around and swim. Me and Arnie. I swam in water that was real, not chlorinated. Swimming outside you can see the trees, so quiet out there.

Now I'm a city swimmer, at night during the summer is best. Look up at the purple black sky, the neon lights of the buildings. Oh, when the moon is up, right over the buildings, that's something. The neon signs just dance on the water.

RUTH

Finished the marathon. I was pleased to have accomplished that. People go on about their times, but for me, it's just about finishing. I met the winner, Kipsang, after the race when all the participants were milling around, greeting and congratulating each other.

"You did great," Kipsang said.

"Thanks. So did you," I said laughing. "Congratulations."

"Thank you. Have you been training a long time?" he asked.

"Several months, at least for this race. What about you?"

"My whole life."

"Good thing you won," I said. "Wouldn't want you to have wasted your life. Do you race often?" I don't know why I said that or asked him that dumb question. It was clear he was a professional, but I have a tendency to get nervous and behave strangely in front of men I'm attracted to.

Kipsang pointed to his shoes. "My sponsor," he said. "I train in France."

He's a professional athlete from Kenya. Usually, I don't go for African guys, they can be a bit macho for me, but he was different.

After the race a bunch of us went out to eat and we sat next to each other. He's left-handed and I'm right-handed so we kept touching elbows which was nice, really. He kept apologizing and I kept telling him that it wasn't an issue and then, somewhere towards the end of the evening, our elbows were touching and neither one of us was moving away.

"I'd like to see you again," he said. He's off for another series of races in Europe where he's sponsored.

"Oh, sure," I said. I looked at his left earlobe.

"Can I come to visit you? I have a holiday coming up."

What could I say? "Sure," I said smiling. I couldn't stop, I'm dreadfully obvious when I fancy someone.

"Do you have vacation time?"

I nodded and suddenly got really chatty. Next thing I know, I'm blabbing about my vacation time, running, holidays, traveling, my family.

They televised the marathon; my big embarrassing moment as the camera was on me while I was walking instead of running. People saw, including my boss.

"I saw you on television. You were wearing too many clothes," my boss said.

I thought Janice was going to have a heart attack. "That's what you wear for a marathon," I answered. Later I said to Janice, "He expected me to wear a short running top and shorts."

"What were you wearing?"

"Leggings and a T-shirt. I had my running bra on. It's not a fashion parade. I know what he wants and I'm not here for that."

Later my boss tried to explain himself and went off on this tangent about sponsorship advertisements and how leggings absorb sweat—to cover up what, as Janice said, was a completely inappropriate statement. Everyone on my team heard his comments. Charlie's ears burned red and Janice almost spilled her coffee.

"He says too much," said Charlie before turning back to his computer.

Janice began to call our boss The Pervert whenever he was out of sight. The Pervert this, The Pervert that, The Pervert wants so-and-so. I told her she'd better stop or she'd have the entire office calling him that. She's half my size and twice as loud.

After my boss made his huge blunder, he told me I had to do a site inspection on Sunday. When I asked, due to all of the overtime these past months, if and when I was going to get my salary reinstated, which would effectively be a raise, he had the nerve to laugh.

"Why should you get a raise?"

"Because I'm the only damn person who can do this job in this entire company." I was calm when I said it, but we're past the point of being polite to each other.

"The economy. No can do, Ruth." Hong Kong has tanked, it's true. Everyone's heading to Shanghai. I threw him a look. "You have to give me some reasons. Put it together in a package I can present," he said reluctantly. He knew what I said was true and he was worried. He has to ask the higher-ups, but it's doubtful that they would know what to say or do anything.

I need this job now. I have bills to pay. But I've got to look around for something else.

The old man with the brown trunks helped me with my breathing and as a result I made it two-thirds of the way across. Funny, those old guys. I quite like them. I went early in the morning and he was there with his friends. He gestured to have me try the crawl by the side of the pool, and I went about ten feet and he told me not to bend my legs so much when I kick. He also told me to pull my head to the side.

I tried to do what he said, but didn't seem to get anywhere. I shook my head and said I was tired, told him I would try again and he said I need to try to move along with it, and not fight it so hard.

With broken Cantonese and his broken English and lots of pantomime, I got it. When I went back in, my stroke was better. I felt lighter and when I surfaced the old man smiled and told me to go home and rest. I told him I had to go to work and he told me to think about swimming at the office. If I did this, he joked, I may not do so well at work, but my swimming would improve. Let the rhythm and feeling dive into your bones, let the water do the work—I knew that was what he tried to convey through his gestures. I can do it when I run, but when I swim, something else takes over.

I remember floating in college; my first boyfriend Dan firmly holding my back as I kept insisting that I sank, that I was not meant to swim. He encouraged me slowly, holding me up, first with both hands, then one, then just a few fingers, lightly touching my back, so I could barely feel him. Then one day, it happened, he let go and I was floating. Just knowing he was there gave me confidence. The fact that I swim at all was due to him. We broke up as all people do in college, over some silly jealousy or misunderstanding. At forty-one, the reasons you have at twenty-one for ending a relationship seem irrelevant, expectations change.

I don't rely on anyone, though I'm not sure if it's by choice. Last time I was Stateside I had heard he was divorced with two kids. I had thought about calling him, but never did. I was too busy coping with my father's death, my mother's mourning and my marriage that had collapsed.

I remember stepping off the plane for my father's funeral, touching ground in the U.S. for exactly six hours before meeting up with twenty-two family members, none of whom had ever flown before and were extremely nervous about getting on a plane to Jamaica. All of us going back to bury my father. The funeral was the last time I cried over someone. *Don't you bury me in the U.S.,* he had said. *I lived here sixty years, but home is Jamaica. That is where my bones will rest.*

FROGGY

After one good lesson, she improved, but there must be something going on. If possible, she's gotten worse the last week. She's not getting any farther. She's splashing around, not concentrating. If I knew English, I might have yelled at her, told her to keep her legs straight and not to flop around so much. Breathe evenly. That's what I tried to tell her before. Nothing worse than to watch someone with potential mess up. She's trying too hard, it happens.

When Man Ho was first learning, he would get it really fast. Then for several weeks he seemed to get worse. Couldn't figure it out.

"What's wrong with you," I asked him. "You forgot everything we did just a week ago?" He shook his head. He was small, maybe seven years-old—a little boy. "How come you forgot?"

"I can't remember," he said to me tearfully.

"It's because you're thinking too much. What are you thinking about?"

"Nothing," he said, shaking his head.

"You have to be thinking about something. Don't think so much when you're swimming. Then your body can remember."

That day he didn't swim well. But then a week later, he was swimming better than he had his entire life. I was so proud of him. I couldn't help it. I taught him. He's my son.

RUTH

I thought my boss was going to lose it.

"You can't quit," he said loudly. He looked upset.

"Of course I can quit. And I am quitting. One month's notice as required."

"I was going to talk about the raise," he said quietly.

"You mean reinstating my salary, or a raise, on top of that."

"A raise."

"I'll think about it," I said enjoying every second of his anxiety.

"You're a good worker, important to the company," he said. As if that meant I was one. I am not a happy Mao worker, or even a happy capitalist worker. We done left the plantation. Christ. But, I admit, I am thinking about it, in a vague distant way you think about a job that you no longer want.

FROGGY

She did it! I knew she would. She got in the pool as usual and started swimming; even kicks, a powerful pull, but without using too much energy, she was just turning her head enough to get some air.

When Ruth hit the halfway mark, even Arnie and Fei Yun stopped jabbering about the gambling cruise Arnie wants to go on. Her swimming was confident.

"Hey Froggy, I think she's going to make it!" said Arnie. "Want to bet?"

"No, I don't want to bet you fool. I've been telling you she's going to make it from the beginning," I said.

"Her technique is better," said Fei Yun. "Slightly."

When she touched the end of the pool we all started clapping and cheering. Congratulations! Well done!

She started crying.

I thought Fei Yun was going to start bawling himself. Arnie handed her a towel. Some of the other guys who've been watching clapped too and came over to offer her congratulations.

I was so happy. I said, 'Congratulations!' about six times. This is an Olympic length pool; not everyone can make it across.

The black woman, the American, her name is Ruth.

Next thing she has to learn is a flip turn. It's fine for old guys like me or Fei Yun to touch the side, though even I do some flip turns now and then. But Ruth's young enough to do a proper turn when she finishes a length. That's the best way!

I should ask Man Ho to come swim with me. We don't see each other much and I bet he hasn't swum in years. He golfs. What kind of exercise is that? Riding around in a cart, hitting a little ball and then eating and drinking afterwards until you have to undo your belt. Bad exercise I tell you, from the looks of him. Whenever I see him, he's gained more weight. It'd be a shame if he never swam again, he was a fine swimmer.

RUTH

I bought my ticket, one way to India and I told Janice to come over to my flat as I was getting rid of my things.

"Here. My very favorite ultra-sexy top. Very small on me, but on you, it'll be bigger. Still it's sexy, don't you think?" I held up the lacey purple top and Janice took it and put it in the corner with the other stuff I had given her. A few Balinese bowls, knickknacks from Thailand, baskets, and blank photo albums.

"No, I can't take that," Janice said when I gave her a necklace of glass beads.

"Why?"

"You told me a long time ago your husband gave that to you. It's sentimental. You have to keep that."

"Janice, I divorced him."

"So maybe you had some good memories."

"Some. Very few. And I can remember them fine without this. Besides, it goes with the purple top."

"Did he give you the purple shirt?" she asked with surprise.

"No. But it goes. He liked me wearing purple. It's really not my color. I feel like a big grape when I wear it. If you don't take it, I'll toss it. I'm trying to start over."

"Okay, okay. Ruth," she said hesitantly. "I wish you good luck. You think you'll come back to Hong Kong?"

I didn't know how to answer her. I will never live here again. She looked at me hopefully. "I'll be back to visit. Hong Kong is inside of me," I said patting my chest. "It's there and has me—inside. I'll come back."

"Hong Kong will miss you," she said. We hugged good-bye and I waved as she walked out to the minibus. She was happy for me, but I felt sad. Truthfully, it will be a long time, if ever, before we see each other again.

I'm good at moving and leaving. In a few months Hong Kong will seem like a long time ago. I have a few contacts, but haven't made any plans and don't know if I'll stay there long enough to get a job. I'll be meeting Kipsang in India after his race in Thailand. These goals you have, ticking them off as the years pass, you begin to wonder why the rush, what is it all for? My father's favorite topic for discussion the last ten years of his life was not just his, but my non-existent pension plan, and he undoubtedly would be turning in his grave right now. *What's your plan? Where are you going?* Fair enough. Good questions.

But I swam my lap. The old men clapped and cheered and I started to cry. I was so glad I made it across the water. It's a very long swimming pool.

FROGGY

When Man Ho showed up at the pool I was surprised. I told him I'd be there in the morning, but I didn't really expect him to show up. I was pleased but tried not to let on how happy I was.

"Should we swim a lap?" he asked me.

"Go right ahead," I said. "Think you remember?"

"My body remembers."

When Man Ho jumped in, I thought he'd empty the pool! This is what happens when you try to swim when you're that big. I hope he keeps exercising. I worry about him and I'm too old for that. He's supposed to be worrying about me!

I swam a few laps and he was there, right at my tail. This means I'm either swimming fast for an old man, or he's too fat to keep up. Maybe he's just letting me lead the way for once in his life.

"Do you want to race?" I asked him.

"I never race when I know I'll be beaten," he said smiling.

My son is an excellent swimmer.

Willow Springs Books is a small literary press housed in Eastern Washington University's Inland Northwest Center for Writers, in Spokane. The staff of Willow Springs Books is comprised of creative writing graduate and undergraduate students. As part of an internship for which they receive college credit, the students get hands-on experience in every phase of the publishing process. Willow Springs Books' staff oversees the annual Spokane Prize for Short Fiction competition. They also publish annually one surrealist poetry chapbook.

Willow Springs Books staff who contributed to this book include Lauren Hohle, Kim Kent, Jess L. Bryant, Myles Buchanan, Matthew Darjany, Benjamin Ganynor, Charles Vaught, and Thalon Hansen.